OVER THE

CW00500850

An exciting new part of her life begins when Nurse Jennifer Turner first reports at the Princess Beatrice Hospital—but nothing works out as she'd dreamed after she meets handsome registrar, Nicholas Smythe.

OVER THE GREEN MASK

BY

LISA COOPER

MILLS & BOON LIMITED
London . Sydney . Toronto

First published in Great Britain 1981
by Mills & Boon Limited,
15 16 Brook's Mews, London W1A 1DR

Australian copyright 1981
Philippine copyright 1981

ISBN 0 263 73568 0

Set in Monophoto Baskerville 11 on 12 pt.

Made and printed in Great Britain by
Richard Clay (The Chaucer Press) Ltd.,
Bungay, Suffolk

CHAPTER ONE

JENNIFER TURNER shook out the folds of her new dress and ran her fingers over the crisp fabric. Not the sort of dress she usually wore, but one that filled her with more excitement than if she had been given an expensive outfit from a leading couturier. She wouldn't have changed the simple cotton-polyester material for the most exclusive fabric obtainable. How funny I must look, she thought with a smile, standing here in black nylon tights and a bra and pants.

The dress felt cool to her burning cheeks as she slid the sleeves over her arms, the collar of the dress was white and close-fitting under her very attractive cleft chin. After a bit of a struggle, the new silver buckle slid into place and she pulled the loose folds of the dress into position, half proud, half frightened of her reflection.

The pale blue of the dress looked clean and business-like and she picked up the tiny cap of folded linen-finish paper. It was so inadequate if it was to cover her hair. She viewed her long honey-gold hair with distaste, ignoring the warmth and highlights and the soft swirls of shadow over her shoulders. For once, she wished she had short dark straight hair that would be easy to arrange. Now, the problem would be just how much she dared show under the cap.

Mrs Bunch, the linen keeper, had been very definite about her hair. 'I can see you having trouble with all that, Nurse. If some of the sisters catch you with hair hanging down, you'll be in trouble, I can tell you.'

'But what must I do?' she asked.

'Hair mustn't touch the collar, Nurse. It's a rule at Beatties.'

'But when I came for my interview, I saw lots of nurses with hair that came quite low down.'

'Not wearing pale blue, you didn't. More senior nurses use their own discretion, and I don't believe you saw anyone looking untidy, did you?'

'No . . . I suppose not.' She recalled one sister who had long dark hair plaited and smooth, although the hair must have hung naturally past her shoulders. 'I can put it up somehow, I suppose. I'll have to practise,' she said lightly, but she was about to report to Sister Tutor in the preliminary training school, dressed properly for the first time in full uniform and her heart sank. Suppose she couldn't get the grips to hold? All the time she was thinking, her fingers were deftly transforming the loose silky hair into a neat French pleat. She brushed as she arranged and the result made her smile. I look a different person, she thought. So demure, so solemn, so dedicated . . . and someone had called her 'Nurse'. It may have been Mrs Bunch, but it was a heady moment. She put a new ball-point pen and pencil in her top pocket, made sure the pendant watch hung straight on her breast pocket and found a clean hanky. Her new cloak, dark blue lined with red, was blissfully warm to face the chill of a murky day in early summer, and who knew what in her new career?

On her list of instructions, she had been told to report in uniform in the main dining room of the hospital, ready to meet the senior nursing officers and the sister who would take charge of the new batch of nurses and teach them the rudiments of hospital procedure and some simple routines before they were let loose on an unsuspecting public. It was slightly unnerving to walk into the crowded dining room, alone. She stood in the doorway and wondered where to sit.

'All new nurses to see Sister Jones at the end table, over there,' said the dining room assistant detailed to direct the shy new arrivals.

To her relief, Jennifer saw that there were several other girls wearing pale blue, already sitting at the table. She helped herself to a tray and joined the self-service queue at the assistant's direction, but looked glumly at the array of sausages and tomatoes or scrambled eggs and bacon offered. 'There's tea in the urn and you help yourself,' called the woman, and bustled away to collect the plates left by early risers. Jennifer took a plate, a roll and butter and jam.

'Are you new, too?' A bright voice cut into her thoughts and she turned to see a pretty, plump girl with red hair who smiled in a friendly way. Jennifer couldn't believe that this self-assured young woman was new to Beatties, or to give the hospital its right name, the Princess Beatrice Hospital. 'This is my first morning. Do you have to report to Sister Jones and then go to preliminary training? How did you like your bed? Mine had a dip in the middle. I wonder who I ask about changing it?'

Jennifer was shaken. Imagine even *THINKING* of complaining about something the moment she arrived!

'I don't know,' said Jennifer weakly. She followed her, taking food that she didn't really want, but bemused by the forcefulness of the other girl, who said firmly that she intended stoking up for the day and took sausages and egg and bacon, complaining that everything she enjoyed eating had far too many calories. 'I don't know if I can eat what I have here,' said Jennifer.

'All right for you. You're so slim, you could eat double helpings and it wouldn't make any difference. I'm hoping that this job will make me so worn to a shadow that I'll look like you. There's a couple of seats free at the end. Come on.'

Jennifer sat down and looked at the food on her plate. She sipped the rather strong tea and crumbled a roll, letting her bacon grow cold. The bread seemed to stick in her throat and she drank more tea. Everyone was eating or talking, with not a glance to spare for the girls who sat at the end table, covertly looking at one another to see if there were any potential friends. It was like being a new girl at school all over again, just when she was convinced of her own maturity.

'I'm Kate Minter. I left school ages ago with seven "O" levels and two "A" levels. I went into advertising, but I found it dull. I've always had a feeling I'd like to be a nurse, so I ignored all my family and said I'd have a bash at it. I can go back to advertising if I can't stand it . . . or if they can't stand me,' she said cheerfully.

Jennifer was so relieved to find someone starting on the same day that she began to tell Kate about her home in the old house in Dorking, her brother and parents. The bread stuck again as she remembered Twig, the black labrador who had whined as she went down the drive, as if he knew that she would be away for a while. A wave of homesickness came over her.

'Come on, Jen. Snap out of it. Of course you're fed up and far from home. I know I'm older than you and have been away from home for some time but, if you can believe it, I'm scared stiff. I talk a lot when I'm frightened and at this moment I'm probably grinning all over my silly face as if I hadn't a care in the world. Well, I'll tell you something. If that door was nearer and I wasn't dressed in this ridiculous get-up, I'd be heading for the smoke and Fleet Street.

Jennifer saw that Kate's large, well-shaped hands were trembling. She took one and squeezed it. Suddenly, she felt better and the excitement returned. 'It's going to be all right, Kate. I feel it in my bones, as my granny used to say. Do you think we'll work together? That would be fun. At any rate, we can meet off duty . . . if you'd like to . . . compare notes. I liked it at the interview and I'm sure we'll like it when we've got over these butterflies.'

Butterflies. She'd had them fluttering in her stomach when she knew she'd been accepted, and she'd had them even more when Nigel had told her that she would never stand the pace, never survive the long hours, never be able to watch people in pain. He had called to see her the day before she left, accusing her of running away from him. She recalled the sulky fire in his dark eyes, the petulant curve of his mouth and the anger in his voice. 'I know you, Jen . . . you'll be back home begging me to take you on again after a few weeks.'

'I wasn't aware that you'd "taken me on", as you so delicately put it,' she said. 'There's nothing between us Nigel, and you know it.' She clenched her hands. 'Just because I enjoy your company, most of the time, it doesn't mean that you own me.' The fact that her parents were great friends of Nigel's family didn't help. From all sides, over the last few weeks, she had sensed disapproval and the effort to discourage her from doing the one thing she wanted, to become a nurse.

'You liked me well enough after the disco,' he said when they were alone and he tried again to take her in his arms. 'What's got into you, Jen? You let me kiss you, and I thought I was home and dry.'

'A kiss at a party, when everyone was kissing because it was New Year's Eve, means nothing,' she said for the fifth time. 'Michael kissed me and you kissed his fiancée and it didn't mean a thing except to say Happy New Year.' She sighed. 'You must leave me alone, Nigel. I'm very fond of you, but I'm not in love with you. Anyone would think that one kiss gave you the right to think of us as engaged.'

'And so it does. I love you, Jen, and I shall have you sooner or later, so why not now? Give up this stupid idea, get engaged on your birthday and we could be married next year. I shall have a job on the coast . . . you'd like that, and in any case they want a married man as games master.'

'Did you tell them that you were engaged?'

He had the grace to look embarrassed. 'Well, if you must know, it was one of the things they wanted, so I said I would be getting married before long. Have a heart, Jen, I *had* to say it. It's a co-ed school and they have to convince the parents that I'm not likely to rape their precious daughters.'

'So you used me . . . how many others have you told about our engagement? It would be nice to be consulted; a girl likes to know what's in store for her, even when she has no intention of falling in with your arrangements.'

She closed her eyes, trying to forget the scene that followed, when she had recognised Nigel for the spoiled, almost violent man he could be when provoked. She ran her fingers along the line of her forearm that still held traces of the bruise from his iron grip as he forced her to turn to receive his kiss. Was she running away? Was Beatties a refuge, a kind of sanctuary . . . a nunnery to which she ran from his clutches?

'At least I shan't have this kind of treatment there,' she'd almost spat at him as she had tried to forget the softer side of his nature in case he could influence her when they calmed down. The high-ceilinged dining room was solid and, instinctively, Jennifer knew that she was safe until she went home again.

A sister approached the table, a chart board in her hand. She called the names on her list and, as each girl answered, glanced sharply at her face as if to imprint the name and face on her memory for future reference. 'Ah, you're all here,' she said. 'I'm Sister Margaret Jones, your tutor for the next month in preliminary training. As you all know, we use the house up the hill and come back here to sleep in the Nurses' Home. Today, and when you are off for whole days, you can have meals here but the rest of the time you will eat in Grey Stones.' She smiled. 'We have a qualified domestic science girl there and a trainee dietician, so we do very well.' Her smile was cool but reassuring and the eight girls who followed her out along the road, selfconscious in their new uniforms and feeling vulnerable to the gaze of the outside world, began to relax.

'Why do we live away from the hospital, Sister?' asked Kate when they reached the steps leading up to the pitted oak doors of the rather ugly house.

'There was a house in the grounds that we used, but there was a bad fire and it had to be pulled down. Its future is still under discussion, so meanwhile we have to be content with this place. It has its advantages and disadvantages. It's peaceful and the rooms are big enough for lectures and demonstrations. In fact, the medics keep some equipment here . . . a few skeletons for first year students and spare wall charts.' She led the way into a light room on the first floor. 'This is where we do most of our practical work, but you will go to the hospital in twos and threes to watch real trolley laying and see how to approach real patients. I have tried to get this done for a long time, to make sure you are used to the wards before you are expected to work there. The medical students do this so I see no reason why student nurses should not share the privilege.'

The new girls followed her meekly as she pointed out the various cupboards and explained what they contained. 'This is your first day. I shall leave you for an hour, to get to know names and to gossip.' She smiled. 'You'll do it in any case, so I might as well get out of your way.' Her smile faded. 'But let's not misunderstand. You will also become acquainted with the contents of each cupboard, each drawer. Tomorrow, woe betide any nurse who cannot instantly bring me what I require when I call for it. You are going to call me hard and very fussy but, in time, you'll see the reasons behind everything you are taught here.'

She stuck two notices into the criss-cross tapes on a notice board. 'This is a list of your off duty for the next two weeks, and that one is a list of the tasks you will perform when you do not have a general lecture. Punctuality is essential, quiet dignity is something to which you will aspire and utter cleanliness is required at all times. Any questions?'

Jennifer was silent, but two girls asked about minor points and Kate asked if she could complain about her bed. Sister glanced at her list. 'You are . . .?'

'Kate Minter, Sister.'

'*Nurse* Minter. When you answer a telephone, or tell your name to another member of staff, you say Nurse Minter. When you talk among yourselves, you will use surnames only in front of patients and you will find the habit stays, off duty as well. You do not tell your names or life histories to patients, you do not speak to the medical staff on the wards unless spoken to first, and then you are brief and as professional as possible. Is that understood?'

'Don't we have any fun?' whispered Kate.

'Nurse Minter . . . you have fun in your own time. You can do as you wish in off duty time, just so long as you bring no disgrace to your uniform or to Beatties. No one talks shop away from the hospital. That is a rule.' She looked from one face to the next. 'That may sound old fashioned and unnecessary, but to illustrate just how important it is, imagine yourself a relative of a very sick patient . . . someone with a very rare and interesting disease. You visit the hospital and see your loved one. You are worried and as you go home on the top of a number nine bus . . . or whatever, you find a couple of new nurses from Beatties sitting behind you. They have heard of the rare case, they know very little about it but, being new, they think they know all the answers.' She smiled rather grimly as they laughed. 'Yes, you'll think that during the first few weeks and then, gradually, you'll begin to see just how little you or anyone else knows about a great many subjects. Back to the bus . . . these two hopeful miracle workers chat and chat about the case, throwing in their own quite dangerous theories about possible treatment, and the relative is left shaken and convinced that everything that could be done is not being done. Do you begin to understand?' They nodded, and Jennifer felt rather deflated.

'By all means talk shop in your bedrooms, and in this lecture room while you are practising your bandages, but never, never in public or on the wards where cleaners and relatives may overhear something not intended for broadcasting.' She looked at her watch. 'The morning has flown. Look at your list and you will find that you are off every evening this week. This afternoon, you will do as I suggested, get acquainted with the place and with the equipment, and keep an eye on the noticeboard by the hospital entrance and the one in the Nurses' Home. There's a disco in the medical school to which you may go if you wish . . . but no fraternising in students' bed-rooms.'

'When is it?' asked two of the girls eagerly.

'In two days time. Now, don't get bowled over by all those clean-limbed young men in white coats. It's all window-dressing, believe me. They know as little as you do.'

'All of them?' Kate looked innocent. 'Even the qualified doctors?' Sister gave her what can only be called a dirty look. 'I mean, have we come to the right hospital, Sister?'

'Make no mistake, Nurse Minter. The Princess Beatrice is one of the finest in London, in England and possibly, in the world.' Her voice was quiet but Kate blushed. 'It is a privilege to train here, Nurse. Anyone who takes the training lightly should go away now, train at a lesser place or give up any idea of becoming a nurse. To some, nursing has become a job of work but I hope that when you see the work done here, nursing will be a labour of love at the highest level. There will be times when you are over-tired and wish you had become a chemist or a teacher or anything but a nurse and then, one day, you will be confronted with a situation that needs you . . . you and the skill you have been taught here, and there will be no doubt in your mind. You will then be a nurse and you will never be quite the same again.'

She relaxed and smiled. 'And as for meeting anyone of importance in the medical world here, forget it for a while. I'm afraid the mere sight of a pale blue dress worn with that particularly inadequate cap will make consultants ignore you or treat you as less than the dust,' she said cheerfully. 'They will look on you as the menaces you will be for the first few months and I can't really blame them.'

'Sister?'

'Ah, Nurse Minter, you asked me about you bed in the Nurses' Home.' She smiled. 'Sleep on it for a while. In time, it will seem the softest couch you have ever had. I promise you.' She chuckled. 'Now, I'm going to the main block for lunch, but you will eat here. After lunch, there will be a few errands to be taken to the main building.' She glanced round the room, and pointed at Jennifer. 'Please say your name when you know I want to speak to you. I shall soon get to know you but it helps if you prompt me.'

'Jen . . . Nurse Turner, Sister.'

'After lunch, take that package to Ward 2. If Sister is off duty, leave it with the staff nurse on duty. Ask her to make sure that Sister sees it as she badly needs it. I bought some new belt ribbon and she asked me to get some for her from this special shop. It's very good and doesn't crumple up like the cheap ones do.' She pointed at one of the others.

'Nurse Marne.'

'Well, Nurse, I believe you have done some

nursing in a psychiatric unit. Do you think you'll like it here?' She looked at the rather solemn woman, a few years older than the average girl beginning her training at Beatties. She looked quiet and self-effacing and rather sad, Sister thought. 'Would you go to Casualty and take back this stick? I borrowed some for a demonstration but Sister wanted every stick and walking aid handed in as they are very short of them. The trouble with equipment like this is that the public seldom remember to bring sticks back when they have finished with them. They seem to think we have an inexhaustible supply and that they aren't needed again.'

Sister left and, after a moment of near silence, a buzz of conversation began with names being exchanged, first impressions compared and a general warming up of contacts. 'Better?' said Jennifer.

'Much better, but I shall have to be careful,' said Kate. 'I say too much. I'm so used to the free and easy relationships of the big city that I shall have to be careful not to seem too familiar.'

They went down to lunch and found that the cooking was very good. 'Quite a little family. Can we have you to cook for us when we go into the wards?' said Kate to the young catering officer. 'How long have we got? Are we allowed out without a chaperone? Can we go across to the main building?' One of the girls who had an older sister who trained at Beatties explained that they could go back to the main block when they were off at lunch time, so long as they were back to report for lectures. They could collect mail and go to their rooms, but it was strictly forbidden to go down the hill to the shops while wearing uniform.

'You have to go over . . . Can you look for any letters for me?' asked Kate. 'I feel lazy. I'll watch the passing scene and ponder.' She sighed. 'I'm tired already, and we've only been here for one morning.'

Jennifer picked up the package and went across the wide driveway leading to the hospital. She looked at the direction board to find Ward 2 and followed the drive until she found the right arrow pointing to Wards 2 and 3 and Minor Theatre, Minor X-ray and Stores. Once more, she was almost overwhelmed by the huge building and by the busy figures who all seemed to know exactly where they were going. Would she ever be like them? The nurses who seemed to drift along on a tide of efficiency, the solemn-faced young men with stethoscopes hanging nonchalantly from the pockets of white coats, who *must* have been at Beatties for ages.

Ward 2 had an aura of controlled haste as Nurse Jennifer Turner peeped through the round spy window of the double doors. She ventured inside and found a side room in which there were several shelves packed with large Winchester bottles of different coloured fluids, some of which were labelled 'poison' and Jennifer recognised as being types of well-known antiseptics. Covered trolleys lined the sides by the sterilising unit and a nurse dressed in a white gown and mask was taking instruments from a boiling steriliser and putting them on a towel-lined tray, using long-handled forceps.

The nurse saw her. 'What do you want?' she said shortly.

'Sister Jones asked me to give this to Sister,'

said Nurse Turner.

'Put it in the office. I'll see she gets it tonight and . . . Nurse . . .'

'Yes . . . Nurse?'

'Is there a ward nurse handy?'

Jennifer looked out into the ward but her view was obscured by two lines of cubicle curtains. She could see no other nurse.

'You'll have to help,' said the staff nurse. 'Don't look so scared. Just put on a mask and do as I say . . . I only want something from a sterile drum and for that you have to wear a mask before you open it.' She was speaking with the patient concentration of someone talking to a fool. 'You have worn a mask before, I suppose?'

'No, Nurse. I only came today. This is the first time I've been to a ward and that was only to bring the parcel.'

'Ye gods! Masks are in that packet. Take one and put it on; and hurry, for heaven's sake, he'll be here at any moment.'

With trembling hands, Jennifer took a folded mask and tied the tapes behind her head in the same position as the ones on the head of the staff nurse. The edge of the mask cut into the bridge of her nose where she had tied the tapes too tightly, but she dared not adjust it more comfortably. 'Which drum, Nurse?'

The staff nurse waved a pair of forceps in the direction of one of the larger drums. Jennifer opened the top and held the lid by the top handle, realising that she must not touch the sterilised contents. The nurse took out a bundle and placed it on the tray.

'Good, now lower the lid, gently and make sure it is firmly shut.' She quickly spread a sterile towel from a small open drum on to the tray, covering it completely, put the forceps back in their antiseptic holder and, without a backward glance, picked up the tray and hurried towards one of the curtained cubicles.

Jennifer put up a hand to untie the mask and found that, in her agitation, she had turned the bow into a tight knot. That's all I need, she thought.

'Leave it,' a deep voice said. 'Come on, follow me.' He scowled at her over his green mask. 'Why is it that everyone disappears when I need a nurse?'

'But I'm not on this ward,' said Jennifer.

'Then where are you?' he said sarcastically. 'Not the ghost of the proverbial Beatties grey lady, are you? Hurry up, but first, take that packet. We'll need that. The vein's collapsed and I may have to tie in a canula.' He held his hands chest high and Jennifer saw that they were encased in shining rubber gloves. He's scrubbed up, she thought. That's why he can't touch anything. A hint of excitement grew and threatened to make her lose her cool. 'Yes, that one,' he said. He paused. 'Is there a needle and two canulae in there? I might have to try one of two methods.'

Jennifer undid the tapes of the sterile pack and opened it. She saw several wrapped items inside.

'What the hell do you think you are doing? Are you a complete lunatic?' Too late, Jennifer gazed horrified at her very unsterile fingers probing the contents of the pack. 'Do you realise that you have just unsterilised the last cutting-down intravenous pack on the ward? Get another . . . get out before I do something for which I probably would *not* be sorry when I get my breath back . . . and Sister shall hear of this.'

Jennifer tried to speak, but the fury in the dark brown eyes terrified her. She put the pack down on a bare spot on a draining board and fled. There was nobody in the ward to ask, nobody in the sluice room. She nearly ran to the office and saw a student writing notes. 'Where do I get a cutting-down set? It's urgent,' she gasped.

The man started up. 'I'll get it,' he said . . . 'Don't cry . . . please don't cry. It's only our surgical registrar being Olympian. Get back into your hole, little mouse, and come out only when he's calmed down.'

Jennifer didn't need telling twice, she ran along the corridor and bumped into the ward sister coming back to Ward 2. Sister told her off for running and asked who had told a first day probationer to put on a mask in the main building, and when Jennifer blurted out the whole sad story, she tightened her mouth.

'It's not your fault Nurse. My Staff Nurse had no right to ask you to help, and as for Mr Smythe, he should know better,' she said softly. 'Take off that mask and straighten that silly cap and tell Sister that I kept you. I shouldn't talk about this to anyone, as I think it unlikely that you'll meet Mr Nicholas Smythe again for a long time, by which time you will both have forgotten that this happened. You will forget, Nurse?' It was an order.

'Yes, Sister. I will forget it,' she said meekly. She knew it was easy to promise something, but could she keep that promise? Would she forget the fury in those dark eyes? Would she forget the strength of those broad shoulders and the unexpected grace of his gloved hands? Dark eyes . . . Nigel Croft had dark eyes, but his held cruelty in their depths. Even when Mr Nicholas Smythe was angry, the dark eyes gave a hint of another fire that could engulf any woman unwise enough to come into range. His dark eyes were quite, quite different and, when her panic subsided, Jennifer decided that in anger they were far more appealing than the dark eyes of love which Nigel sought to use to bring her to him in marriage.

CHAPTER TWO

SISTER JONES tapped on her desk for silence. 'I don't mind you talking, but I can't hear myself think. I have a report to write but I keep hearing fragments of quite fascinating conversation and find I am listening to what is no concern of mine.' She looked rather pointedly at one of the girls who had been recounting a blow by blow account of a date with a dental student friend of her brother's. 'I shall come round and inspect those bandages in just five minutes and, from one casual glance, I wouldn't pass any of you if it was an examination.'

Jennifer sighed. Her hand was rapidly becoming numb under the tight folds that Kate had enthusiastically applied. 'Can't you loosen it? My arm's dropping off. I'm sure that it shouldn't look like that either.'

'You can't talk. I can hardly hear you.' The mastoid bandage that Jennifer had put on was thick and had twice as much material in it than was necessary, while tufts of red hair sprang out of every gap like a fiery weed.

Kate giggled. 'We wouldn't be any good in an emergency yet, would we?'

The door opened and the class of nurses gasped. A tall figure leaned against the doorpost, a sardonic smile giving a wicked expression to his handsome face. He glanced round the room and let his gaze dwell on Kate's bandaged head. His eyebrows shot up. 'A very bad case, Sister,' he said. Jennifer turned away to the old-fashioned bandage roller which was still very useful for re-winding bandages used during practice sessions. She could feel the blood surging in her cheeks and dared not look at the man who had been so rude to her in the clinical room of Ward 2.

'Well, Mr Smythe, to what do we owe the honour of this visit?' Sister's voice was controlled but guarded. 'As you can see, we are very busy.'

'I'm sorry, Sister. I didn't come to waste your time, although it all looks ... fascinating.' He grinned. 'I've been roped in to give some lectures to the third year student nurses and I wondered if you had a store of old equipment that I can use for demonstration purposes.' He was serious. 'I'm glad to see that you teach the basic skills even if they aren't used very often in hospitals like Beatties. That's why I want the sort of aids that could be applied in a more primitive environment.'

'I'm glad you said that, Mr Smythe,' said Sister. 'Listen, all of you.' Jennifer turned her face towards Sister, hoping to remain unseen by the visitor. 'One day, any of you may come across a situation where there are no plasters, no special aids and you will have to use any material at hand. There will be no tubular bandages, no stick-on dressings, just old linen torn from a table cloth or sheet, and you'll have to bandage with that. The same applies with any of our sophisticated equipment that you will learn to take for granted as you use them every day on the wards.'

'I did a stint in domiciliary midwifery and, believe

me, nothing can be as primitive as that, in a poor area.' Sister was looking at him with growing approval. 'I expect you know all about that, Sister?' he said. She nodded. 'It taught me that we must adapt our treatment to what is available, make everything as clean as possible, sterilise instruments carefully and have faith, lots of faith.' He smiled and every girl in the room smiled back at him, except Jennifer. He's nothing but a spoiled Casanova, she thought. He's trying to charm everyone in the room. Well, I know what he can be like. I know how horrible he can be to a person whom he had no right to ask to help him. And didn't Sister of Ward 2 say he shouldn't have asked her to help him?

A ripple of amusement ran through the class. 'Don't you think so, Nurse Turner?' said Sister.

'I'm sorry . . . I . . .' Jennifer looked blank.

'I'm sorry, I must go. I realise that there might be some who don't share my warped sense of humour,' said Mr Smythe. He was looking at her intently, with a slight frown, as if he was trying to place her. Thank goodness I was wearing a mask when he told me off, she thought.

Sister led him away to the store along the passage and as the door closed behind them, a buzz of excited speculation broke out. 'Isn't he a poppet?' said Penny Mason, the youngest of the group, a girl from a sheltered, vicarage background who was ready to like everyone who crossed her path.

'Not a poppet . . . oh, no . . .' said Kate. 'Get those Mephistophelian eyebrows! That man has more to him than that.'

'I know, I think he's horrible,' said Jennifer.

'Oh, no!' a chorus of denials came from the rest, and it was evident that Jennifer was the only one who had any doubts about his attractions.

Sister came in and released the girls from their various bonds. Jennifer flexed her numb fingers and Kate disappeared to the cloakroom to tidy her red hair and to put her cap on again. Jennifer began to roll the bandages again, as it was her turn to make sure that everything used was ready for the next class. One nurse was detailed to do this after each lecture and, after bandaging, the rolls seemed endless.

'I can imagine him,' said Penny, with stars in her eyes. 'I can imagine him in some tropical island where nobody has taken the benefits of church or medicine, healing and comforting and bringing civilised ways of life to backward groups of people. He wouldn't need all the expensive trappings that some doctors think are essential ... he'd manage with ...'

'A stick or two, some sea water and a monkey to help him, I suppose,' said Kate dryly. 'Be warned, my innocent young friend. That man could be dynamite if he chose.' She glanced at Jennifer. 'As I believe at least one of our number has discovered already.'

'No,' said Jennifer, in a panic. 'I don't know him, but I disliked him, that's all.' Sister had told her to forget that she had met him and, in any case, she couldn't bear to let the others learn of her humiliation. 'There are some men who repel me,' she said, 'and Mr Nicholas Smythe is one of them.'

'How did you know his name, if you have never

met?' asked Kate softly.

'Sister said it,' said Jennifer, but Kate smiled slowly, knowing that his first name had not been mentioned.

'Nicholas . . . it suits him,' said Kate '. . . quite a bit of Old Nick about him, I shouldn't wonder.'

The class proceeded with a demonstration of bed-making. Sister regarded them all before she began. At first, they all looked alike, but now, the different personalities were emerging. The last batch of new nurses had been, dare she even think it, a little heavy going, but this crowd looked as if they would be a challenge, a headache sometimes and a pleasure. They had a certain spark that she liked to see. The others had been good workers, easy to handle and a credit to her teaching, but with them she had missed something. The faces in front of her might be solemn when she told them what she wanted them to do, but their humour and vitality showed through. Perhaps I shall wish I had a more stodgy bunch before we've finished, she thought.

Kate gave an impish smile. 'I can make a bed, Sister.' Sister Jones took a deep breath. It was starting already. She turned away for a moment, so that the girls couldn't see her smile. 'May I try?' said Kate.

Sister led them into the practical room where there were two beds, an enormous cupboard in one corner and a skeleton hanging from a stand, bony feet just touching the ground and one arm raised as if in salute. The grinning skull was tilted to one side, giving it a very knowing expression.

Sister stood at one side of a bed and motioned

Kate to stand opposite. She briskly stripped the bed and put the folded bedclothes across a chair. 'Right, Nurse. You say you know all about it, proceed to make the bed.' She beckoned to Penny. 'You help her, but let her tell you what to do.'

Kate pulled at a sheet and, in her sudden nervousness, pulled a blanket with it and dropped it on the floor before Penny could dive for it and save it. Kate bent to pick it up and leaned on the chair, sending it over. A moment later, the bed clothes were all on the floor, the heads of the two nurses came together with a thud and Nurse Kate Minter landed in a heap with the clothes on the floor. Sister stood calmly watching the mess. Jennifer ran forward and helped to fold the sheets again.

'Now,' said Sister, when the clothes were across the chair again. 'Shall we try again, but slowly?' There was a twinkle in her eyes.

Kate smiled sheepishly. 'I'm sorry, Sister. It's quite obvious that I can't make up a hospital bed, quickly.'

Sister turned to the others. 'Your first lesson wasn't bedmaking after all. It was something far more important. Never mind admitting that you are wrong. If you make an honest mistake and admit it, nobody reasonable will blame you. In our profession, it is essential to avoid making mistakes, but if you do make them, you must do everything in your power to put matters right, or tell someone more able to do so. Remember, you have no time for your own false pride when a life may depend on your ability to admit a mistake. Now . . .'

The class continued and when they had all

managed a bed without too many loose ends, Sister handed a key to Jennifer. 'I can't imagine real patients being very comfortable in the beds you have made, so we'd better have Arabella. Will you fetch her, Nurse?'

Jennifer blinked and looked at the key. 'Arabella, Sister?'

'It's all right, Nurse, I haven't gone mad. Arabella is our dummy, and the only patient you will touch until you pass your test in the training school. Arabella has had a very painful operation . . . say an operation for removal of gall stones. She must be moved gently at all times.'

Arabella was large and floppy, with woollen hair of a slightly mangy tom-cat colour. She had a very silly expression.

'She's not very pretty,' said Jennifer.

'Some of your patients will be quite repulsive, nurses, but you must treat everyone alike, with care and courtesy.' There was a lot of laughter as the dummy was manoeuvred on to a bed and the class ended on a note of hilarity.

The door opened and Claire, the trainee dietician, came in with a huge jug. She put it down and went back for mugs and biscuits. 'Cocoa,' said Sister. 'I'll leave you to tidy up and write up your anatomy notes before lunch.'

'It seems we've been here for ever,' said Jennifer, sipping the hot cocoa. 'I think that if I have to roll another bandage, I'll go spare. Thank goodness we take it in turns. As for that awful grinning dummy . . . I'd like to strangle her.'

'Worse to come, I believe,' said Roberta Marne.

'We have to learn to give her an enema, blanket bath her and introduce a catheter.'

'Oh, *no*,' said Kate. 'I bet she leaks.' The atmosphere during the two days that they had been in Grey Stones had warmed and it seemed impossible that they had all arrived at Beatties as strangers. In that short time, they knew about families, friends, who had a regular boy friend, who was engaged and who wanted to dedicate herself to a life of service. 'Let's pop across to get a breath of fresh air and see if the post has arrived before we start on our notes,' said Kate.

The plane trees were in small leaf, a wisp of white cloud beyond the laundry chimney was the only blot on the clear blue sky and the birds were singing. 'It would be nice to walk over the Surrey Downs,' said Jennifer. 'It seems miles away.' But she said it with none of the longing she felt on her first day at Beatties. Home was another dimension, another life, and it was only when she saw the familiar handwriting on the envelope that she gave a thought to Nigel. She thrust the envelope into her pocket with the letter from her mother and waited while the other girls found theirs in the pigeon holes inside the small office in the Nurses' Home. I suppose I ought to telephone or write, she thought, but couldn't think what she would say if she did. All the things she had done during the last two days were not the sort of activities that would interest them. An anatomy lesson, bed-making and bandaging, a few talks and . . . that awful time in the clinical room in Ward 2.

'Hello, Mouse. Got over your shock? Old Nick didn't put you off nursing for life?' The voice was warm and full of laughter, and Jennifer smiled up at the sturdy, good-looking man with the level grey eyes who had sympathised with her and helped her.

'I didn't have time to thank you,' she said.

'Think nothing of it. I have a talent for helping damsels in distress. I'm Charles Bird, in my last year before finals. And you?'

'Nurse Turner,' said Jennifer.

'Brainwashed already? Not allowed to reveal your true identity?' He lowered his voice to a whisper and looked about them with exaggerated suspicion. 'Come on, tell me, and I promise not to split on you.'

Jennifer laughed and her laugh was more spontaneous than any she had managed for a long time. 'Jennifer,' she said. 'You are an idiot.'

'Well, I like that. No gratitude.'

'Are you coming back or shall I go on?' called Kate from the drive.

'I'm coming,' said Jennifer.

'And my reward for letting you off the hook?' Jennifer paused, her hand clutching her cap. 'You have to dance with me tonight. You are all coming, I hope?'

'See you,' said Jennifer. She raced after Kate and then slowed to a demure walk as she saw the green of a sister's uniform.

'You know him?'

'No . . . I met him when I took the message for Sister,' said Jennifer.

Kate looked sideways at her. 'Busy little . . . mouse, aren't you. One man you haven't met but you know his name, and the other calls you Mouse after a brief encounter and asks if . . . Old Nick upset you . . . my, my, we have a mystery woman on our hands.'

Jennifer blushed deeply. 'Sister told me to forget what happened, but I have to tell someone.' They walked slowly back to write up their notes and as the others had gone ahead, Jennifer could tell Kate about the incident without the whole group hearing. 'So now you know why I took a dislike to your wonderful Mr Smythe,' she finished.

'Some people do lead the most exciting lives,' said Kate.

'You won't say anything to the others?'

'No, I promise, but be careful. If a man like Nicholas Smythe took a dislike to you, it could make life difficult here. On the other hand . . .' She gave a wicked grin. 'I can't think of a better way to force him to notice you, if that's what you'd like. Perhaps I should slip on a banana skin at his feet. He has that remote look when he's not talking, that means he isn't interested in us . . . or he has a woman hidden away at home.' She shrugged. 'He is just too good-looking for words. He's probably married with a clutch of children.' She frowned. 'I thought he looked sad just now.'

'Just now?'

'You were much too busy putting your head close to your new friend to notice. He was watching you as you stood in the doorway . . . and I think he recognised you.'

'Oh, no . . . I was wearing a mask when he swore at me. I know he didn't recognise me in the class room.'

Kate walked in silence, then said slowly, 'It was as if he recognised you from another place. As if you revived an old memory . . . a sad one.'

'He was probably cross.'

'No, not that. Somewhere, he has seen you before, or you remind him of someone he hasn't forgotten.'

'I didn't see him.' Jennifer felt a sense of loss. But she didn't want to see him again, did she? She brought her mind back to the open face of Charles Bird, the first man at Beatties to show an interest in a new nurse. 'I'd almost forgotten the disco,' she said lightly. 'Charles Bird asked if we were all going.'

It sounded as if she was passing on a general invitation and she wanted to keep it that way. 'I doubt if we shall see Mr Smythe at anything so ordinary,' she said. 'I imagine his scene is the bright lights of the West End . . . cabarets and luscious blondes.'

'But you rather wish it wasn't?' said Kate.

'No . . . of course not,' said Jennifer. 'I don't like him. Charles Bird is much more fun.'

'Je crois,' said Kate cryptically.

'I think you fancy him,' said Jennifer, in an attempt to take attention away from herself.

'Not my type,' said Kate. 'I find that I'm not at ease with all this attention to seniority. In my job before I came here, there was a kind of hierarchy, but not like this. I see the value of knowing who knows more than who, and there must be someone to give orders and know that the orders will be carried out, but it was all so relaxed . . . hectic, but very relaxed. In time, if I stay, I might like the clear cut differences and be able to accept that I do not speak to dishy men unless I'm spoken to! I can't imagine going up to Mr Smythe in a pub and saying I admired a layout he'd done.' She giggled. 'What am I saying? His layout would be on an operating table, not an advertising project.'

The day passed slowly, now that they weren't doing something as a group, but merely writing up notes and looking up references in the rather battered nursing manuals in the small library. There were books on every aspect of nursing and they made Jennifer realise just how much there was to learn and how little she knew. It was as Sister had said . . . at first they thought it would be easy, but even one subject was showing signs of having its difficulties. Two girls were disconsolately trying to identify bones on the skeleton, which helped them not at all, but grinned derisively and dangled the limbs they wanted to prop up, refusing to be placed in any particular position. 'You and Arabella make a good pair,' said Penny. 'Not a brain between you.'

At lunch, Jennifer asked if the others were going to the disco. She was relieved to find them all so enthusiastic. Her own desire to go made her wonder if it was the music and dance she wanted or was it that she wanted to see Charles Bird again? He was so different. When she compared him with Nigel Croft, the man who was so determined to marry her, she smiled. Charles had gentle eyes and a warm manner. He was the kind of man who would make any woman feel cherished, even if it was only for the passing moment. He was like that to everyone, she was sure, and it would be pleasant to have his company as a friend. Nigel? She put a hand in her pocket and drew out the letters.

'Haven't you read your mail, yet? I can never wait to open mine,' said Penny. 'Anything interesting?' she said, with her usual guileless curiosity.

'Only from home,' said Jennifer and opened her mother's letter. She sat in the small sitting room of Grey Stones, as they waited for Sister to arrive. As usual, Mrs Turner wrote as if Jennifer had done something very rash. If I'd joined the Parachute Brigade, she couldn't be more shocked, thought Jennifer. It was as if the letter had opened the door to a distant past, but it had been only a few days since she saw her home and family. The gap was widening and letters such as the one she was reading would do nothing to bridge it. Her mother complained that she had to arrange the church flowers alone, that Jennifer's father was always out on business and that Dear Nigel was missing his girl friend very much.

'Dear Nigel . . . she would say that! Anyone would think we were married,' said Jennifer crossly.

'Not another man?' said Kate, who was sitting, draped over the arm of a deep chair, her tiny cap at a perilous angle. 'Tell me all . . . if there's time. We only have five minutes before Sister comes. Come on, I'm all ears.'

'So I noticed when I tried to bandage them,' said Jennifer sweetly. 'It's a boy from home . . . no, not a boy. Nigel is very much a man of the world, I suppose. His father is an estate agent and a very successful one.'

'Special?'

'Not as far as I'm concerned. He's very dynamic and persistent but, frankly, I was very glad to get away for a while. Unfortunately, Mother likes him and thinks he would be the perfect husband for me. Together, they thought they had it all sewn up.' She looked grimly at the other sealed envelope. 'I can guess what's in this one, from him.'

'Well, you shouldn't go round with swathes of beautiful hair and that fine skin: your eyes aren't bad either. I know someone who would pay you to do commercials for eye make-up.'

'You have to be joking,' said Jennifer. 'You heard what Charles Bird called me? Mouse . . . the first thing that occurred to him.'

'You were scared out of your tiny mind, weren't you? Not at your brightest, at a guess. A mouse, yes, a smooth, sleek little mouse, with that hair in a roll, but I should wear it like that if you want to keep Charles . . . or your friend Nigel, in order. Loose, it really is very good . . . shining, no split ends and that lovely colour. Michael would give anything to have you on his books.'

'Stop talking about me as if I wasn't here. You'll have me advertising dog meat next.'

Kate laughed. 'Old habits,' she said. 'Now tell me about Nigel. Do you dislike him, or are you putting on another act?'

'Another act? I wasn't aware that I'd put on any act, at all,' said Jennifer. She looked perplexed. Was that what Kate, her new friend, thought of her? That she was shallow and light, encouraging every man she met? She gathered her letters together, the one from Nigel still unopened, and rose to her feet as Sister came in to collect her charges. Kate couldn't think that. She was teasing. There had been only the letter from Nigel and the meeting with Charles Bird. She firmly tried to forget the anger in the dark eyes under the devil's eyebrows. That was not a friendly encounter, and never could be.

'This afternoon, we're going down to Surrey in the mini-bus.' The girls exchanged pleased but puzzled glances. Anything would be better than another session with Arabella or Jimmy the skeleton.

'Do we go in uniform, Sister?'

'Yes, Nurse Marne. You wear those dresses and put clean ones on tomorrow morning. We must be fairly hygienic, both where we are going and afterwards.' She smiled. 'We are to visit a dairy farm and study milk production and its care, from cow to consumer.'

'Sounds like a commercial coming up,' whispered Kate.

'In cotton dresses, we needn't bother the farmer to supply us with overalls . . . not for our protection as much as an assurance that we don't take infection to the milk.' She laughed. 'It becomes uncertain who is contaminating who, after a session there, hence the fact that we send everything we wear to the laundry afterwards.' She glanced outside. 'I don't know if you've had time to notice, but the weather seems settled and it's going to be really warm. Leave your cloaks in your rooms and just bring a cardigan or a light sweater in case you need it. Meet me at the lodge in ten minutes.'

'Do we have to milk a cow?' said Penny apprehensively.

'That should please you,' said Kate. 'Back to

nature and all that . . . we could include an ad. for substitute butter at the same time. Anyone mind being photographed with a cow's back-side?'

Jennifer picked up a blue cardigan which was pale enough to go with her uniform. She left the letters on her bed and once more put off the act of slitting the envelope bearing Nigel's firm handwriting. It will keep, she thought, and wished that he would give up.

'You were telling me about your love life,' said Kate when they were in the small bus, feeling like children on a Sunday school treat.

'I wasn't, because I haven't any,' said Jennifer.

'Je crois,' said Kate.

'Why do you use that irritating little French phrase?' said Jennifer.

'Because it expresses my delicate disbelief without actually saying "you liar". I know of three men already.'

'Don't be daft . . . I met Charles twice, very briefly, and he invited us *all* to the disco, and I've told you I'm not in love with Nigel. You should learn to do sums, dear, that's only two . . . unless you count that dreadful porter on the lodge gate who wants to know everything about everyone. I think he's a spy. He probably has a dossier on every member of staff,' she said.

'Claud has his uses. He's good for stamps and information about theatres . . . and gossip . . . lovely gossip. I adore him. He's so revolting.'

'I had noticed that you are almost as bad as he is! Well, what do you want to know? You might as well hear the truth instead of a garbled account from your bosom friend in the lodge.'

'Do you really dislike Nigel or is it all a ploy to make him all the more eager?'

'Nigel is a man who usually gets what he wants, but he uses methods that many people find unacceptable.' She sighed. 'Daddy has never been the "go-getter" that my mother would have liked. He likes to take time to stand and watch the flowers grow . . . you know. He is a vet in a small town and makes a comfortable living. But he'll never move away and, sometimes, my mother gets very fed up with the local scene. In a way, I suppose people like him are as selfish as the Nigel type, but at least he's warm and loving and I know that, basically, my parents are very happy with their marriage.'

'That disposes of your father . . . what has it to do with Nigel?'

'I've heard that he is a very hard business man, like his father. I've heard several people say that if they wanted to sell a house, they'd go to him, but if they wanted to buy . . . they wouldn't touch his firm. He gets the last penny, by one means or another. Nothing illegal, but it leaves a nasty feeling that he has not acted quite fairly, in certain cases. He's young, but he's making a lot of money.'

'And that's bad? Where were you brought up? In cloud cuckoo land, dearie? That's business. It's a hard and often dirty game and everyone accepts it. He sounds ordinary enough to me. Is he physically repulsive?'

'Oh, no,' said Jennifer. 'He's very good-looking, in a way. Dark brown eyes and good features . . . hard features. Quite tall and plays rugby and wants

39

to teach games.' As she talked, she knew that she was telling the truth, but she was unable to convey what she felt like every time she was with him.

'Your Mr Smythe has dark brown eyes, good features, and I think is the type to play rugby,' said Kate.

'But not like Nigel . . . he . . . oh, nothing, and I wish you wouldn't try to read something that isn't there. They aren't a bit alike. If I really knew Mr Smythe, I might find he was even worse than Nigel, but not being in his business, at least he wouldn't think that having put a deposit on an article, it gave him a right to possession.'

'Cryptic, too,' said Kate. 'One kiss and he thinks you ought to go shopping for the bed?'

'Something like that,' said Jennifer. 'And I don't want him.' She recalled the barely controlled violence under the charm if everything didn't work out for Nigel Croft. She also had a fleeting vision of two mobile eyebrows raised in mock alarm when he saw Kate with her red hair emerging from the untidy bandage. Mr Smythe had humour, somewhere lurking beneath his arrogance, even if she personally never came within reach of it. Soon, he would remember that the inefficient junior nurse was the girl with tightly pinned hair in the lecture room, and he would avoid her like the plague.

For a moment, she looked sadly out at the tree-lined road.

'Nearly there,' said Sister.

'We're just outside Epsom, aren't we? I thought I recognised the road.'

'Yes,' said Roberta Marne. 'I used to work in one

40

of the psychiatric hospitals here.' She seemed suddenly pale.

'What was it like?' asked the girl sitting with her.

'I just want to forget it,' she said, biting her lip as if she wished she had kept quiet about any old associations.

'I thought you said you nursed in Liverpool,' said Kate.

'That was after . . . it doesn't matter. I did work in Liverpool,' she said firmly, in a voice that encouraged no further questions.

'The dairy belongs to one of the hospitals. They try to make the long-term patients self-supporting and so they have a dairy, a market garden and a laundry where those who are able, work and earn pocket money. It's a controlled but imaginative environment where they can know they are doing a useful job and have security. They may not be able to face the complicated life they would meet outside the hospital, with forms to fill in, food to buy and rent to pay, so this is an answer, even if it isn't ideal.'

They drove under a heavy stone archway where thick double doors were flung back against the high walls to allow traffic to enter. 'Protection . . . but also a prison,' said Nurse Marne softly. 'I couldn't stand it. I had to get out. There are nurses who love the work and are valuable, but the ones like me who felt imprisoned are no help to the patients, the system or the other nurses.' She tried to smile. 'Beatties was a revelation to me after . . . that.'

They gazed up at dark stone walls and barred windows and wondered how a building in such beautiful gardens could be so cold. 'Make no mistake, I'm not against the work they do. I admire everyone who can work there, but I was too weak.'

'It takes a strong person to admit to her own weakness,' said Penny Mason piously.

'My dear girl, you don't know what you're saying,' said Roberta, and hurried after Sister who was waiting to usher them in to the farm office.

'Your own stamping ground, isn't it?' said Kate.

'Not quite,' said Jennifer. 'It would have been terrible if we'd gone on this mystery tour only to end up on my own doorstep.' She giggled. 'It would serve Nigel a lesson if I took you all in to his office in uniform when he had an important client to see.' Her smile faded. Epsom wasn't very far from Dorking and the small village outside where she lived . . . as the crow flies, or as the estate agent travels.

The dairy proved to be very interesting and rather sad. There were several anencephalic patients with the small slanting head typical of the congenital condition which robbed the infant of most of the brain and left the child unable to fend for himself as he grew. These sub-normal humans were pathetic, abandoned by family, dependent on institutions and having no hope of improvement in their intelligence. 'They're like zombies,' said Kate.

'The ones born without any brain at all, die at birth, I believe,' said Roberta. 'But some have a little brain and a great hold on life. They grow up like that and can do simple tasks . . . one task each, over and over again. Other patients were working quite well and the stalls and milking parlour were clean and well kept. The cows seemed to like their keepers and this, at least, was a happy place, with pride shown by the men and women caring for the herd.

Kate made an attempt to milk a cow but after she had been swiped by a less than clean tail, she gave up and the laughing farm manager couldn't persuade another to volunteer.

'We arrange tea in Epsom after this trip,' said Sister. 'There's a rather nice café with an upstairs room where we can have our tea without half the population thinking we are the entertainment for the day.' They followed her from the mini-bus into the café, past the enticing display of homemade cakes and buns and up the broad wooden stairs.

Penny Mason went to the window overlooking the High Street and looked out at the sun shining on the mixture of old and new which made Epsom a lively and interesting small town. Jennifer swivelled round in her chair while they all waited for the tea to arrive, idly looking at the shop signs, the pub sign on the corner and a hanging coat of arms which announced that a shop sold goods 'By Appointment' to a royal personage. The next shop had another hanging sign. It was an estate agent.

Almost as she realised, a man emerged from the doorway, glanced up to see if the day was still fine enough for him to leave the light coat he carried over his arm, and saw her. Too late, she turned away, hoping that she was not recognised, but Penny laughed and said, 'I think he thinks you gave him an invitation, Jen. That man is coming into the shop.'

CHAPTER THREE

'SURPRISE, surprise,' said a sarcastic voice over the telephone line. 'I made it and I decided that I can come, tonight.'

'You've got a nerve,' said Jennifer. 'I told you quite firmly before I left home that I wanted time to get used to Beatties and that I wouldn't be seeing you for at least a month. Don't you realise that I have work to do? Notes to write up? I can't see you, Nigel.'

'But that nice Sister invited me. Seemed very pleased to think that a boy friend of one of her flock could come and console the awful feeling of loss and homesickness you must be suffering.'

'You conned her into believing that you were my fiancé . . . she told me. Why didn't you come upstairs and ask me if I wanted you to come tonight?'

'Give me credit for more sense, my love. If you had met me then, the thunderclouds would have told Sister that all was not sweetness and light between us and she would have hustled you out of my clutches, clucking like the proverbial hen. All I did was to ask if she knew Miss Turner, who had started at Beatties last week . . . no, I wouldn't stop to embarrass you, but it would . . . sob, sob, be good to see you again.' He laughed, triumphantly. 'She thinks I'm very charming, very much in love and will be an asset to any party. Right on all counts, of course.

You never told me that boy friends would be welcome at your little jollies.'

'Boy friends, yes, but that rules you out, Nigel, after the way you behaved the last time we met.'

'But I did say I was sorry.'

'When?'

'You haven't read my letter? Naughty girl, it's all there. I even said I was coming to London soon, but this afternoon hastened my visit.'

'Nigel . . . I need time to get used to this place. It's taking all my time and concentration to do my work and to know the others. If you must come, can't you leave it for a week or so?'

'That's just what I have no intention of doing. The sooner you realise that you are being extremely foolish, and come home, the better. Your mother agrees with me. She's ready with list poised to send out the invitations.' His voice softened. 'You know how much I want you, Jen . . . and if this absurd bug hadn't bitten you, we'd have been married by now, living in the old manse. I bought it for a song and I'm quite prepared to spend a small fortune on getting it as you want it. I'll give up the idea of teaching.'

'Sell the damned place and don't come here tonight, because I'm not going. I'm going to the pictures!' She slammed down the telephone. 'Damn Nigel, damn Sister for giving him this telephone number.' She looked round for some other person or thing she could damn, but the hall was empty. She went listlessly up to her room. He would spoil it all. The other girls now believed that she had a good-looking fiancé who was coming to the medical school

45

disco tonight, she had told Charles Bird that she would be there and she couldn't see a way out. If I don't go, Charles will be insulted, and he was very kind. If I don't go, Nigel will send one of my friends to find me and make a fuss, trying to sound as if he was worried.

'Coming out as far as the lodge?' said Kate. 'I have a few letters to post and Claud promised to get me a paper.' She frowned. 'You all right?'

'Nigel rang and swears he's coming tonight.'

'Well, why worry, safety in numbers. Just show him that he's not the only man around and if he gets stroppy, tell him to jump in the river.'

'You don't know Nigel,' said Jennifer weakly. 'I go through all that when he's not here, and when I see him, my courage evaporates. He can be very pleasant, very charming and very attractive when he likes. He has a hypnotic quality and I feel like a trapped rabbit.'

'Or mouse? You do have another man. Charles looks more than able to look after his own interests.'

'I just wish I wasn't going . . . if I chicken out, will you say I've gone up West to a show? No, I suppose not. It would do if only Nigel was involved, but there's Charles to consider. That man is very sweet,' she said.

'Me, I like my men a bit mean and moody. Charles would bore me to tears after a week,' said Kate. 'Now, him! That man is all hidden fire . . . I'm an expert, I can tell.'

'Who?' Jennifer looked up from the strip of stamps she was folding away in her purse. Mr Smythe was walking quickly towards the main block, dressed in a white coat, and he was hurrying. The expression on his set face was rather like the one he had when she opened the sterile pack. 'I'm glad it isn't me this time,' said Jennifer, but wished that she could follow, to watch what he was doing, to see him again, at close range, even if she was burned by the contact. 'I wonder what's happened. He seems busy.'

'Well, even if he is a disco dancer, which I doubt, he can't have time for such frivolity tonight, that's certain. He is Surgical Registrar on 2, isn't he?' said Kate.

'Yes, I think so. He seemed quite at home the day I made a fool of myself.'

'Well, that's why he's busy. Claud said Ward 2 were taking emergencies tonight and there's been an accident on the motorway. Listen.' The distant sound of an ambulance came through the dull blur of normal traffic. A police siren cut through the mild air and the blue flashing light on the car roof came in an arc as it drew up at the entrance. The two girls were drawn instinctively to the doorway, wide eyed.

'Do you know, we could do nothing if we had to cope with that,' said Jennifer. 'Where would you begin?' They stood to one side, keeping well out of the way as trained ambulance men opened the rear door of the ambulance and slid the stretcher from the smooth runners inside the vehicle. A still form, draped in a red blanket, was followed by a man clutching his head and writhing in pain. There was blood on his face . . . lots of blood, but the still pale face was much more terrifying. 'Is he dead?' whispered Jennifer, and a slight movement, less than a sigh, seemed to say that there was life there, if it could be saved. Porters ran with the trolleys and the ambulance men began to clear the soiled blankets from the back of their vehicle, bundling them up and taking them to be exchanged for clean ones. One man tested the oxygen cylinder, the first aid box went for re-packing and there was an air of quiet efficiency which restored everything to normal, ready for the next emergency.

'How can they just get on with the cleaning up as if it was water and not a man's blood that was spilled on the floor?' said Kate. But Jennifer had been watching the casualty nurse who came out, took one look at the casualties, listened to a few terse sentences from the police sergeant and went to the internal telephone, calling to her juniors as she hurried away to cut away the clothing of the man with the ashen face and not to move him.

'She knew what to do,' said Kate. She turned shining eyes to Jennifer. 'It's that sort of thing that makes me feel an utter fool, but makes me certain that I want this more than anything I've wanted in the whole of my stupid, useless life so far.'

And it was with that much conviction that Jennifer decided about Nigel. She had only to think of the scene outside casualty to know, like Kate, that this was the life she wanted, and that Nigel hadn't a chance of making her change her mind.

Kate was recounting the scene with flagrant exaggerations. By the time the others had heard it, Kate had, single-handed, taken at least six unconscious men into the hospital. 'Don't leave out the part where they asked you to perform brain surgery,' said

48

Jennifer, and everyone laughed, a trifle nervously. They scattered to their rooms to get ready for the disco. Under the windows of the Nurses' Home, an old car wheezed and almost exploded. Kate leaned out of her window in time to see several young men carrying musical instruments into the medical school. 'Sounds as if the group has come,' she called.

'Charles said it was made up of students,' said Jennifer, bringing in an armful of clothes for Kate's inspection. 'Very good, too,' he said. 'Why must Nigel threaten to spoil it all, she thought. Perhaps even he would have second thoughts about bursting into what was really a private function. It could be a very pleasant evening if he kept away. 'I don't know what to wear,' she said.

Kate pursed her lips. 'If it was a smart do, I'd wear those velvet jeans and . . . yes . . . that shirt is good. Amber silk would be perfect with that lovely hair, if you let it out of that hideous roll.' She laughed. 'But seeing the group, I imagine that this is strictly informal, with jeans, sweat shirts and training shoes!'

'Jennifer produced a tee shirt of blue cotton. 'It's much too warm for anything too heavy, especially if we're dancing. I think I'll wear that. Nigel never liked it, and I suppose it is a bit washed out. He called it my 'orphan Annie' shirt and looked down his nose when I wore it, which pleased Mama as she wanted to throw it out ages ago.' She giggled. 'I think you've hit on the answer, Kate. If I dress like a poor little student, Nigel will be very uncomfortable. In fact, knowing him, he will arrive in very smart clothes. He is used to more high-powered company than we find in the medical school.'

'They do look terrible, or most of them do, but somehow . . . right, and I like the style, or lack of it. It proves that they have more important matters on their minds. They don't care how they look. I suppose they blossom into reasonably dressed human beings eventually, but I find them refreshing after the trendy bunch I'm used to in advertising. I have the feeling that it doesn't matter how much or how little money I have, but people here will judge me for myself and what I have to give of . . . me.'

'There are a few smartly dressed doctors,' said Jennifer. 'One of the consultants was in the corridor and looked fit for a garden party.'

'That would be Sir Horace . . . and you weren't far wrong. Didn't you hear that he was going to lunch with a Royal . . . He's female surgical, you know.' She smiled.

'Now, *that* would impress Nigel, so please don't tell him. I think I'll wear those trousers. They match the washed out tee shirt. Shall I leave my hair? I know that Nigel has never seen it like this apart from the glimpse he had of me at the café window.' She eyed the smartly understated silk jump suit that Kate took from her own wardrobe. 'I shall feel like your poor cousin,' she said. 'I hope I don't put everyone off as well as Nigel.'

'There won't be anyone to impress. Charles has seen you only in uniform, so he knows what you look like with hair screwed up.'

The beat could be heard well down the drive as the 'Beatties Boneheads' tried out a few routines. Kate began to gyrate as she approached the entrance to the medical school and Jennifer had misgivings about her own appearance. She could imagine what Nigel would think and say. She shook herself. That was the object, wasn't it? To show him that she mixed with a rather scruffy set and to let him feel let down by having a companion who couldn't bother to wear a pretty dress or eye-catching jeans as he would like.

The high-walled room, that had been the old refectory and was now a reading room and library, had the book cases set back against one wall to make plenty of room. A buffet was on trestle tables at one end and a small dais supported the loudspeaker system, the slightly sweating musicians and a couple of potted plants. Charles Bird came across the room. 'Hello Mouse,' he said, and Jennifer knew that he saw nothing of the faded jeans and dragged tee shirt, but only her face . . . the real Jennifer. Her heart warmed to him. He was so . . . cosy. With him, a woman would feel safe, patients would have confidence and other men would instinctively like him. 'It's a bit early, but we could have some beer . . . or there's cider.' He went to get drinks for Jennifer and Kate and, gradually, the other medical students and nurses came in. The bar was two deep with men when Charles fought his way through, spilling hardly a drop. He had a tray with six glasses of cider and two of beer.

Kate turned round, pretending to look for the other five people. He grinned. 'I've been here before. Two beers for me, two ciders for you two and extra if any of your set arrive without a bloke.'

'You are the most thoughtful man,' said Kate. She sipped her cider, her eyes searching the room to see what talent presented itself.

'Friend of mine, dying to meet the vision in red silk,' he said.

'Burgundy ... please ... not red,' said Kate. 'I couldn't wear red with my hair.' He raised a hand and two tall men appeared as if awaiting a signal. Jennifer was amused. Kate attracted her own kind. These men were well groomed, dressed in expensive casuals and looked far more mature than the majority of the students. They brought their drinks, sat for a while and without even seeming to ask her, took Kate away to join a group in the corner. 'See you later, if that's all right,' she said. 'If you need help, just scream.'

Charles sat by her side in an alcove made by two book cases. 'I thought they'd hit it off,' he said complacently. 'Now, let's get to know each other.' An hour went quickly, with Jennifer telling him something about her life at home. She hesitated when she thought of Nigel, but decided to tell Charles a little. She hinted at Nigel's possessiveness and the fact that they were definitely not engaged to be married, nor did they have any other deep relationship.

Charles regarded her with a serious look in his grey eyes. 'I think he scares you.'

'No ... not really, but he said he's coming here tonight and I'd hate anyone to have the wrong impression.'

Charles took her hand. 'Dear Mouse,' he said, and she realised with a sense of shock that she might be exchanging one possessive man for another, the only difference being that Nigel wanted to take, with force if necessary, while Charles would swamp her with care and cossetting, expecting and hoping that she would fulfil his 'little woman' image. He also must think that she wanted him to know that with Nigel out of the running, he could step in and take over. She drew her hand away. I don't want to be taken over by anyone, she thought.

Charles was humming contentedly. He pulled her to her feet. 'Dance?' he said, and Jennifer was glad to follow him to join the dipping, weaving band who did their own interpretations of the dance. 'Not a John Travolta amongst them,' laughed Jennifer, and smiled at Charles as he tried to pick up the beat. She was enjoying herself. If Charles could be like this, amusing and friendly and caring, life could be interesting. But from the glint in his eyes, she knew in her heart that for him, faded jeans and the scrubbed look mattered not at all. He was on the verge of falling in love with her. Why does that worry me, she wondered. Wouldn't he be the ideal man for her? Gentle, considerate, clever, and a good doctor one day, she felt sure. Then why did her glance travel to the door as if someone might come in, or stand there raising eyebrows that could belong to the devil, mobile and expressive, hinting at a sardonic humour, a strong personality and a single-minded devotion to his chosen profession? She smiled brightly, and tried to give her full attention to the dance. It was fun and it was late, and Nigel had decided to leave her alone. The music stopped with an ear splitting discord and the group went on strike until they had replenished their beer supply. Charles was talking to another student and Jennifer smoothed back the tightly coiled hair, tucking in an escaped tendril that curled round her cheek.

Nigel sauntered in and looked about him. Jennifer saw him through the haze of smoke and dimmed lights. He was dressed in a well-cut suit of very expensive cloth. His shirt could only have come from the leading shirt makers who had recently become the trendy house to patronise, and his tie was dull-textured heavy silk. He looked urbane, secure in the knowledge that he was as good-looking as any man in the room and had the indefinable security that success gives to a man's appearance. His gaze wandered, his smile was set.

Penny Mason ran from the side of the bespectacled youth who had confided to her that he wanted to be a medical missionary, and smiled happily at Nigel. 'You're Jennifer's friend, aren't you? I heard you talking to Sister. I know that Jen's here somewhere . . .' She looked round the room, confident that she was bringing two love birds together. 'Half a tick . . . I'll go and see.' She hurried away, intent on being useful, leaving Nigel with a supercilious expression on his face as if he had every right to expect young women to run his errands.

'O.K. I saw him,' said Jennifer. 'Thanks, Penny,' she added reluctantly, wishing the girl would leave other people to sort out their problems in their own way.

'I'd no idea you were engaged . . . you are a dark horse, Jen,' said Penny with a coy glance.

'I'm not . . . and I've no intention of being,' said Jennifer shortly.

'Shall I tell him where you are? I could bring him over,' said Penny.

'I came to this dance with Charles Bird. As far as I'm concerned my date was with Charles and I stay with him. I didn't invite Nigel and I have no wish to see him. So, please . . . don't get involved.'

Penny was flushed with her success at gaining the full attention of a man—a solemn, rather unattractive boy but one with whom she had much in common. It gave her a false gaiety, a recklessness she didn't possess. 'You've had a lover's quarrel . . .' She wagged an accusing finger at Jennifer. 'Come on, now, kiss and make up.' She giggled and ran off.

'Oh, *no*!' said Jennifer. She saw Penny laughing and saying something to Nigel, who treated her to at least a fraction of his strictly rationed charm. He stubbed out a cigarette and walked purposefully across the floor, but he hadn't been listening to the garbled announcements through the badly fitted mike. Floods of dancers were on the floor, all around the elegant figure. Each way he turned, Nigel was impeded by flying feet, writhing bodies and a sheer weight of numbers. Jennifer watched, fascinated as he began to look annoyed, then really cross. He pushed and was pushed back, in good measure, anyone who even noticed how he was dressed thinking he was playing the fool. He was fast losing his temper, his vanity was being hurt and his suit was threatened by the tankard of beer that one student was attempting to balance on his head while he did his own version of the Greek glass dance . . . to a rock number.

Jennifer laughed and Charles saw the cause of her laughter. His lips twitched. 'Let's get out of here,' he said. 'We'll take a walk until he's cooled down. I take it that the sharp dresser is Nigel?'

Together, they slipped through the kitchen at the back of the hall. Charles took her hand and they ran down the drive to the park. Only when they reached the shelter of the trees did they pause for breath. Jennifer leaned against the man who had taken her by the hand like a knight rescuing a lady from a dragon. 'Thank you, Sir Galahad,' she gasped. He put an arm round her and hugged her close. 'You are my favourite mouse,' he said, and released her. And Galahad was the perfect knight, she thought, with an uprush of tenderness. Nigel would have acted quite differently in a similar circumstance.

They strolled through the park. The early summer night was fragrant with the scent of blossom. Pink cherry and almond sprays hung heavy over the gravel paths and the distant traffic sounds were a part of another world. It was warm and peaceful, and they found that they could be quiet together. Hand in hand they wandered, exploring. They smiled at the preposterous stone horses and the slightly battered lion by the ruined fountain. The walks were well kept but the rest was a forgotten garden, full of shrubs and trees that badly needed pruning. 'I hope they don't discover it, but let it stay like this. I can't imagine it full of regimented flowers, neat beds and clipped yew,' said Charles. He seemed content to be with her and to accept her friendship and expect nothing more . . . at this time.

'We'd better go back,' he said. 'I'll go and sus out the land.' He chuckled. 'Would you like me to give an owl's cry or my authentic imitation of a wolf?'

'If you do the wolf call, Nigel might answer it!'

He left her in the shadows by the entrance. She saw couples and knots of people leaving, and heard a roar of protest from the tireless dancers when the group said it was time they packed up. If Nigel is still there, he must come out soon, she thought. The band gave another hint to the hangers-on. They turned all the lights out. Lighthearted shouts and lecherous suggestions came through the darkness. She smiled. It was all good fun . . . all talk, but she knew that if Nigel was still in that room, he would be seething with anger by now, feeling slighted, insulted by the attitude of people who valued the intrinsic merits of a person more than they valued the trimmings of good clothes and expensive cigars.

He could never fit in with them, she thought. He could never be accepted by them and I am one of these people, at Beatties, the place where I want to stay and serve . . . if I'm good enough. She saw him leave, the set of his shoulders revealing a latent violence that made her shiver. She shrank back as he took one last furious look at the building. He walked quickly to his fast car and, in a moment, the red tail lights dipped at the gate, paused and shot away into the night in the direction of Surrey.

She walked unsteadily out into the light of the street lamp by the side of the drive. She sat down on the wall, at the junction of the drive with the spur that led to the brightly lit doorway to casualty. The tension that had been building up since she saw Nigel in Epsom culminated in a sensation of falling. I ought to have eaten, she thought, as swirls of mist threatened to envelop her. I had nothing to eat in the café, I had no supper and we didn't have a chance to have any of the buffet. I'm just low on food. But the lights flashed up and down and round and she slumped to the ground, exhausted, mentally, physically, and drifted into a half-world in which she wanted something strong, someone to whom she could cling and receive some of the strength she had lost.

'Charles . . .' she whispered. She saw the outline of a man coming towards her and knew it wasn't Charles. This shape was different. Tall, and the light from the doorway lit the face and the glint of dark hair. The brown eyes were serious . . . were they angry? Were the dark eyes the ones she had seen full of vicious resentment only minutes away? Nigel had come back . . . and was wearing a white coat. It must be Nigel . . . She began to scream and to beat at the broad chest with feeble hands. 'No . . . No . . .' she said. The strong, implacable hands gathered her into a tight embrace, but instead of the shock and horror she had expected, the arms gave her security . . . as solid as a wall of warmth, of a tenderness she had never dreamed possible.

Jennifer fought for self control and looked up into the face of Mr Nicholas Smythe. Charles was there too. She tried to speak but closed her eyes. She was safe.

'I only left her for a minute,' said Charles. 'Do you think he attacked her? He didn't have time to . . .'

'We'll wait until she's coherent before we call "Rape",' said a cool voice, and Jennifer opened her eyes. 'Do you know her well?' said Mr Smythe. He was walking, carrying Jennifer as if she was feather light.

'She's one of the latest batch of student nurses, Mr Smythe. She was avoiding an objectionable type from her home town and got a bit up-tight about him. I went to see if he had gone and . . . you know the rest.'

'And has he gone?' The voice was clipped, as if he would like to speak to the man responsible for reducing a young nurse to this state of nervous debility. He put the girl on a couch inside casualty and Jennifer saw the stern face relax into a half smile. 'Awake? Are you all right? Any pain?'

She struggled to sit up, but he gently restrained her, his fingers on her wrist. 'I'm fine . . . just hungry, I think,' she said.

'Pulse racing but settling.' He stood over her, against the light, his dark eyes like embers burning away all chance of concealment. 'You should pick your boy friends more carefully,' he said.

'I didn't ask him to come,' said Jennifer. She sat up.

'Your private life is no concern of mine. I understand that you have come to train at Beatties. May I suggest that you keep your own affairs separate from your work?' He frowned as if trying to place her. 'I've seen you before.' His glance took in the shabby clothes, the unbecoming hair style and her pallor and, from that glance, Jennifer gathered that he found her untidy, badly dressed and completely unattractive. He looked away and grinned. 'I prescribe hot toast and coffee, or whatever I can muster in the Nurses' Home. I think that you aren't allowed in that holy of holys after midnight?' he said to Charles.

'No . . . Sir,' he said.

'Then, you'll just have to trust me to see that she gets fed. Can you walk?' Jennifer nodded. Charles raised his shoulders in a resigned gesture and Mr Smythe, sublimely aware that he was pulling rank, walked ahead with a wicked smile on his lips.

'Goodnight . . . Mouse,' whispered Charles. 'I'll ring tomorrow evening.' He wandered away and Jennifer followed the awe-inspiring figure into the kitchen of the Nurses' Home.

'Please don't bother . . . I can make some coffee,' she said, becoming embarrassed.

He raised his eyebrows. 'Don't be selfish. I have to eat, too.' Helplessly, she watched him cut bread and put it in the toaster. He heated milk and produced a pot of strawberry jam from a cupboard and held it up to the light. 'Thieving swine,' he murmured amiably. Jennifer drew her feet together, sitting straight in the chair. Who would dare to borrow jam from Mr Smythe's private supply? Who would dare to do anything to cross him?

He didn't ask her what she wanted, he just handed her a thick slice of toast which dripped butter and jam, put a mug of milky coffee by her side and sat on the edge of the draining board, munching as if he was starving. 'I know how you feel,' he said eventually. 'I was hungry, too. Missed dinner tonight,' he added, wiping a run of jam from his chin. Jennifer found that she, too, had been taking huge bites and was feeling better with each mouthful. 'Now tell me what that was really all about?' he said, and his voice

60

was completely professional. 'Do you feel faint every time a nasty rough man chases you?'

She blushed. He was laughing at her. 'No,' she said. 'I was hungry, that's all, and it's been an exciting day.'

'A trip to the dairy is exciting? Well, well, I must try it, if I can stand the pace. Is that all that happened? I know that your friend arrived and you were less than pleased to see him. Did it upset you that he was discovering you had . . . other interests at Beatties?'

'It wasn't like that. I told him he wasn't welcome. I was not prepared to see him. I told Charles Bird that I'd go to the disco with him.' As she said it, she knew the impression she was giving. She had got her dates mixed and was scared of being found out by her steady boy friend who was rightly angry when he found out.

He turned away. 'I'm not interested in the finer points of your affairs. I am interested in you only from a medical point of view. If you are to train here, you must be healthy and able to give of your best at all times. Nursing is a tough job and takes stamina and strength. We can't have wishy-washy girls who faint in emergency situations.' He paused and the dark eyes seemed to bore into her soul. 'Are you pregnant, Nurse?'

The hot blood transformed her pale face from the apathetic weary impression she gave him to a blazing-eyed, angry girl with a deeply cleft chin that he had not noticed. Her eyes shone with golden lights and her hair, which had suffered from the fall by the casualty doorway, was becoming loose, sending loose curls in clusters round her temples. She braced her shoulders and the firm line of her virginal breasts heaved with angry emotion. 'How dare you suggest such a thing. How dare you.' She stormed from the room, leaving him looking after her. She took with her the humiliation of knowing that he could hardly think any other bad thing about her. She was inefficient, although she wasn't certain that he recalled their first meeting, she was untidy and badly dressed and now . . . she had fainted. So, of course, according to him . . . from his lofty perch in the hierarchy of Beatties' staff, she must be pregnant. The type of girl who slept around and then wondered why her men became uncontrollable.

He sat for quite five minutes after she had gone, frowning.

CHAPTER FOUR

'I'VE visited people in hospital, but this is a different feeling,' said Kate. 'When I visited my uncle, the other visitors looked at me but the patients were too busy seeing what their own folk had brought them to show any interest. Now, though, I feel as if I'm in a goldfish bowl.'

'The pale blue uniform doesn't help. In some hospitals, it's difficult to know who is a junior nurse and who is a staff nurse but, at Beatties, patients learn from their first day that the blue dresses are rank beginners, the darker blue for nurses accepted after preliminary training school and their month's trial on a ward.' Jennifer tugged at Kate's dress. 'Look at Staff Nurse Bond. I think that cap is lovely . . . do you think either of us will ever get to wearing one?'

'Beatties uniform did a lot to convince me that this was where I wanted to train. I love the special Victorian caps that staff nurses wear and those cute bows that Sister Jones has under her caps.' She stood tall as the ward sister came towards them. 'Nurse Minter and Nurse Turner from PTS, Sister,' said Kate. 'Sister Jones said we had to report to you at ten o'clock.'

'Oh, yes . . . I must confess, I'd almost forgotten that you were coming. I'm going off duty, but Staff Nurse Bond will show you the drug cupboard while she gives out ten o'clock medicines and then I'll ask her to let you watch her lay up the dressing trolleys for the morning round.'

'I hope I'm not asked to do anything . . . I'll die if I make a bad mistake again,' whispered Kate as Sister went in search of her staff nurse. She smiled nervously and the man in the end bed winked. She turned away, pretending not to see him. He didn't appear to have much to wink about . . . or to smile about, either. He was thin and his skin was a deep yellow. Even the whites of his eyes looked jaundiced and Jennifer wondered if he felt very ill.

'Come on . . . if you're coming,' said Staff Nurse Bond ungraciously. 'There's a lot to do and I can't afford to be slowed down.' She walked quickly the full length of the ward, with no apparent awareness of the many eyes that watched her progress but, from the elegant straight back, the neat ankles and slim waist, Kate assumed that the lady was fully aware of her impact on every male in sight, however sick he was feeling. The faint resentment that she first caused by her brusque manner, faded. It was evident that she knew her job. The slim, neatly manicured hands manipulated bottles and glasses, pouring accurate and carefully checked dosages. Any drugs marked 'Dangerous', or 'Poison', she checked with the two student nurses, making them repeat the dosage aloud, checking it with the prescription and the note on the patient's chart. Even if three people were on the same medicaments, each had his own separate bottle or container, clearly labelled to allow no room for error.

'Have you learned the common dosages and their abbreviations?' They said that Sister would be doing that later. 'No rush. You will have very little to do with this until you've been here a while.' Her manner was softening, flattered by the close attention and respect that the juniors showed. 'One of you will come to this ward for her month's trial. This is a chance to get to know the place, although you will find that each ward is laid out in the same way as far as drugs and dressings are concerned. That means that you should be able to go into any ward in Beatties, go straight to a drum of small swabs, a drum of intravenous sets or a bottle of spirit. There are large Winchester bottles of commonly known anti-septics and skin preparations, all in the same order, all on the same levels.'

'But wouldn't you like to arrange things as you want them?' said Kate. 'If I was a sister, I'm sure I'd feel like moving things to try out different ways in case I hit on a more convenient way.'

'That's what we have to avoid. Imagine rushing into the clinical room, thinking you can put your hand on a resuscitation tray only to find it isn't there . . . that some bright person thought it a good idea to keep it at the other end of the ward.' She smiled. 'Believe me, if you had Mr Smythe bawling for an injection of Coramine or something similar, and you wasted precious moments, you might just as well give up and go home.'

Jennifer felt her legs trembling. So . . . if he caught her doing anything wrong, just one tiny thing would be enough after her first disaster, then she might as well give up her idea of being a nurse. 'You said one of us would be coming here. Where will the other one go?'

'There are two surgical wards. One general surgery like this and one genito-urinary along the corridor. Have you any ideas of what you would like to do?'

'I don't really mind, Nurse. Do you prefer nursing men or women?'

'I started on women's medical and hated it, but that happens with everyone. The first ward is the hardest and there will be times when you soak your poor feet and wish you had stayed at home and married some nice easy bloke.'

She laughed. 'And now . . . you'll never guess where I want to have a ward of my own, one day . . . women's medical!'

She pulled the screens round the bed at the end. 'Now, Mr Gunter, I'm going to prepare you for this afternoon. Nurse!' she called, 'is my trolley ready?' A junior nurse in the darker blue uniform brought a covered trolley and handed masks to Staff Nurse Bond and the two visitors. Jennifer looked at hers in horror, recalling the last time she had worn one. 'Well, put them on . . . they don't bite,' said Nurse Bond. Jennifer tied hers carefully, remembering to leave it a little looser than on her first attempt. Kate smiled over the top of hers, with sparkling eyes.

'Do we just watch?' Jennifer stood as far away from the bed as the limited space behind the curtains allowed.

'Yes, but if I ask for something outside, go to the nurse you saw just now and she will fetch it.' She glanced sharply at Jennifer. 'Ah . . . I know where I saw you. I had a rocket from Sister about asking you for help.' She stared. 'It's funny what a difference a mask makes to some people. With your mouth and chin covered, you look another person.' She smiled, with a hint of malice. 'I should whip off that mask if Mr Smythe comes in . . . he had a rocket too.'

'Mr Smythe . . . but surely he wouldn't be . . .?'

'You don't think that Sister could give a lecture to a registrar? That's where you are wrong, Nurse. A sister is in charge of her ward and is responsible for her patients. Anyone coming into her ward is a guest . . . even the consultants, however much they throw their weight around once they're here. In the event of an emergency, Sister is held responsible for what happens, so she is rightly able to dictate to anyone who wants to come here. Mr Smythe asked you to do something which was not your job and not within your terms of reference. He should have known by your uniform that you were not able to help him, but he chose to ignore that.'

'What happened, Nurse . . . was the patient very ill?' The thought had haunted Jennifer almost as much as the memory of that furious face when she contaminated the sterile pack.

'As it happened, no harm was done. Mr Smythe was in a hurry to put up a drip before a patient went down to the theatre for a laparotomy. He believed, quite rightly, that the veins were depressed and difficult to enter. He cut down to the vein and tied a canula into position before surgery was started, thus making sure there was a route for saline, plasma or whole blood, as it was needed. But there was no need for panic and he was very naughty.'

'Naughty?' Jennifer couldn't hide her surprise. The thought of anyone calling Mr Smythe naughty was absurd. He was terrifying, but not . . . naughty.

'Oh, dear, Nurse Turner. He really did scare you. He'll be so shocked when I tell him. He goes through life thinking that we all like him for his sunny nature.' The staff nurse's lips twitched. While they had been talking, Staff Nurse Bond had been scrubbing her hands at the sink outside the cubicle. She shook the drips away and dried her hands on a sterile towel. 'I needn't be as fussy as this for a skin preparation in the ward,' she said, 'but you might as well get used to the fact that everything must be pure. Preparations are, in a way, self sterilising . . . or at least self purifying, though the skin can never be really sterile, but we do our best by painting it with one of many skin paints, according to the surgeon's requirements.'

'Well, then, Mr Gunter. Ready?' The junior nurse folded back the bedclothes, exposing the patient from pubis upwards. A plastic sheet was tucked under him, covered with a towel to catch drips and Nurse Bond took a pair of forceps from the tray, held a large gauze swab on the end and dipped it into a galley pot of bright orange liquid which had a rainbow gleam round the edges.

'What's that?' said Kate. 'Is it iodine? Will it sting?'

'I was going to ask that, too,' said Mr Gunter apprehensively.

'Nothing to worry about, Mr Gunter. We thought you'd like yellow to match your skin,' she said lightly. 'It's cold but that's all. It's a preparation of flavine in spirit. I don't even need to put it down below where the barber shaved you. He is a bit enthusiastic . . . we could use a male nurse instead, but the patients seem to like him and he is *very* thorough. To be strictly correct, he would have shaved this area that I'm painting. Now what organs are under here, Nurse Minter?'

'I know,' said Mr Gunter proudly. 'It's my gall bladder, Nurse.'

'The same as Arabella,' said Kate seriously.

'The gall bladder, the liver, the lower ribs and the gut leading from the stomach. All these could be the subject of surgery in this area.' She added more paint and waited for it to dry which it did quickly as the spirit base evaporated.

'Here . . . you aren't taking all that lot out, are you?' said Mr Gunter anxiously.

'No . . . just having a look at the gall bladder. You have some nasty little stones there, which show up in the X-ray.'

'Mr Smythe told me that. He said there might be one blocking a tube and making me yellow. I can't see how that could happen, but I suppose he knows best. I don't remember swallowing any stones . . . where would I get stones?'

Nurse Bond applied the covering dressing, making sure that the painted area was covered completely with sterile towels, firmly fixed in place. She took the tray into the clinical room and Kate opened the curtains to the cubicle. 'It never fails to amaze me how little these people know of their insides,' said Bond, as she washed her hands again. She busied herself laying up a trolley for a lumbar puncture while she talked to the other two who stood away from her as she went swiftly and surely from drum to steriliser, to trolley and back to the steriliser. Everything she did was with a kind of casual expertise, confident that she knew exactly what was needed and wasting no time in doing it quickly and without fuss.

'I can't say I know all that much, Nurse,' said Kate.

'But you would know that it wasn't a stone that you *ate* that ended up in your gall bladder?'

Kate laughed. 'Oh yes, I know that, but how does Mr Smythe know that a small stone is causing the jaundice?'

Nurse Bond finished the trolley and carefully wheeled it to one side, well covered with sterile towels. 'Come into the office,' she said. She switched on the light behind the X-ray viewer and slotted a dark X-ray into position, so that the picture was illuminated from behind. 'Look,' she said. She traced the outline of a shadow filled with what seemed to be dark gravel with smooth sides, faceted to fit against the sides of other particles of the same substance. 'Those are the stones that they will remove. The tiny duct leading from the gall bladder into the bowel sometimes passes small pieces and they are eliminated from the gut. Others may get stuck in the duct leading from the gall bladder in such a way that the flow of bile is stopped, it cannot be passed on into the bowel and gets absorbed into the blood stream and so to the skin. The result is as you see. He has had a lot of pain when small stones were passed down the tiny tube, he has been unable to eat as there is no bile to help him to digest fats and his liver is unable to cope with the bile that is held up.'

'Will he ever be well again? When I first saw him, I thought he was dying,' said Jennifer.

'I think he'll be all right, but they can't tell definitely until they see what's inside. If there was a growth blocking the bile duct, it might be more difficult.' Nurse Bond looked at her watch. 'Did Sister say if you were to go to first or second lunch?'

'First lunch, Nurse Bond. Thank you very much,' said Jennifer. 'I've learned a lot this morning. I can't think that we've been here for only two weeks.'

Nurse Bond smiled. 'Two more weeks and your test. I suppose you are experts at all the things you will never need?' There was a trace of irony in her voice.

'But Mr Smythe said we should learn those things in case we were confronted with a situation when we'd have to use primitive methods,' said Jennifer.

'So you've met Mr Smythe again? You haven't been on the wards before, have you?' her voice was suddenly sharp. 'Did you meet him socially?'

Kate answered for her. 'He came to the school. He wanted Sister to give him some old splints and things.'

Nurse Bond relaxed. 'I see,' she said. 'He has these odd ideas . . . we are always laughing and arguing about them.'

'May we go, Nurse?' said Kate.

'Oh . . . yes . . . I shall wait until Sister comes back before I go to lunch, and help Mr Smythe do the lumbar puncture before he goes to the theatre.' Behind her back, Kate was holding up the mask she had just taken off, mouthing to Jennifer . . . 'take it off'. Jennifer tore at the tapes and stuffed her mask into the soiled linen shute, just before a now familiar figure appeared from the corridor.

'Ah, there you are, Mr Smythe . . . we were just talking about . . . the lumbar puncture trolley. It's all ready, if you'd like to scrub,' said Nurse Bond, with an entrancing smile.

'Hello,' he said to Jennifer. 'Better?' Nurse Bond regarded them with frank curiosity tinged with annoyance. 'I haven't seen you since you shared my toast and you ran out on me.'

Jennifer fled, her face crimson. He was laughing at her. He was cruel to taunt her in front of her friend and a senior staff nurse. What must Nurse Bond imagine had happened from what he said? She now joins the think-the-worst-of-Nurse-Turner-club. I told her that I had seen him in the classroom, or Kate did, and denied that I'd met him socially. It's a wonder he didn't ask if I'd managed to get over my fainting fits . . . or terminated my pregnancy! And how that Nurse Bond could look at him as if she could eat him whole . . . well! Some people needed their heads examining.

'Wait for me,' said Kate. 'You started off like a racing car. What's eating you?'

'Every time I see that man he laughs at me or is so rude he leaves me speechless,' fumed Jennifer.

'He wasn't rude . . . seemed to be just being polite and interested.'

'He was sneering at me. You didn't hear what he said to me after the disco . . .'

'No.' Kate looked thoughtful. 'You never did tell me what happened after Nigel vanished in a cloud of smoke.'

Jennifer blushed as she recalled the cold voice of Mr Smythe saying, 'Are you pregnant, Nurse?' She felt again her misery and humiliation. How could he think that of her? Even though he didn't really know her, wasn't it obvious that she wasn't an easy lay? 'I'd rather not talk about him,' she said. 'I think he's insulting and has a nasty mind.'

'Oh, did he make a pass at you when he was feeding you?'

'How did you know he fed me?'

'I met Charles. He was hopping mad.' She glanced at Jennifer slyly. 'I think Charles had the impression that his lordly registrar was trying to horn in on his date. He told me that Mr Smythe took you off to the Nurses' Home for coffee and comfort.'

'Comfort?' Jennifer nearly exploded with a mixture of anger and laughter. 'There isn't much comfort in that man. He's a bore and a self-opinionated brute.'

'Well, well,' said Kate. 'He did get under your skin. He either tried to rape you or took no notice . . . which was it, little . . . mouse?'

'You're as bad as he is. You're laughing at me, too,' said Jennifer. 'And if we don't hurry, we'll get nothing to eat and my stomach will rumble all afternoon while we do yet more bandages, and make yet more beds.'

'I sometimes think I shall have Arabella haunting my dreams for ever,' said Kate, hurrying to catch up. 'I'm sure that I can do every bandage blindfold and as for blanket baths, if I spill as much water over my patients as I spill over that damned dummy, they'll die of pneumonia.' She laughed. 'We go through all this and yet we can't wait to get into some real nursing ... which is probably much worse.'

After lunch, they reported back to Sister Jones and told her what they'd learned from Staff Nurse Bond. 'I'm glad you saw her,' she said. 'Nurse Bond could do very well at Beatties or any other hospital where she decided to work. I think she will go to another hospital for a while and then apply for green.'

Kate looked puzzled. 'I don't understand, Sister.'

'You've noticed that Beatties sisters wear green dresses? Just as a nurse receives her caps when she becomes a staff nurse, a trained nurse applies for green when she wants to be considered for a sister's post here. But, usually, a nurse who is worthy is *offered* green, but only after she has worked elsewhere for several months.' She smiled. 'After a few years here, Beatties becomes the only place on earth, so it's as well to see how other places cope ... worse in many cases, better in a few. It gives one a chance to have an open mind when dealing with staff from other training schools.'

'And Nurse Bond will be a sister here?'

'Unless she marries a doctor here. Then, of course, she would have to leave or to work in a department where he had no patients.'

'She's very pretty,' said Jennifer.

'Yes, some say that she has her eyes on one of our promising junior surgeons but, as far as I know, it's only a rumour.'

'Mr Smythe,' said Kate, with a knowing smile. Jennifer started. No, she wanted to say, she mustn't. But what did she know of him or of Nurse Bond?

With an unfamiliar sick sensation in the pit of her stomach, she desperately wanted Sister Jones to deny the possibility.

'It might be,' said Sister, with a twinkle in her eyes. 'I'm not saying who, but he *is* very attractive and she is pretty and very efficient, the two qualities most likely to appeal to a man like Mr Smythe.' Sister sat comfortably back in her desk chair. There was a little time before afternoon classes and she found that the two nurses were easy to talk to without losing her dignity as a superior. 'You know that he suffered a sad loss two years ago?' Kate looked blank.

'It's common knowledge, so there's no need for me to try to hide it. When Mr Smythe was doing a house job at Guys before he came back as surgical registrar here, there was a girl there who was very fond of him.' She looked sad. 'I don't know what happened but she was driving with another of the doctors and was killed in a crash. Some say that Mr Smythe was heartbroken and some say that he knew the other man was her lover . . . it all came here as badly distorted gossip and nobody really knows the truth of it.' She paused and glanced at Jennifer. 'I met her once when he brought her to one of Beatties dances. She was pretty, with lovely long blonde hair and the kind of brown eyes that you have, Nurse Turner.'

Jennifer felt icy cold as if a ghost had touched her hair. She knew what Sister was about to say even before the older woman opened her mouth. 'And was he in love with her?' said Jennifer, through dry lips.

75

'I don't know. I think he tried to protect her memory by refusing to talk about her, but everyone knew after the enquiry that she was pregnant. The other man confessed to a friend that he was responsible, but when anyone tried to say anything ill of the dead girl, Mr Smythe refused to comment, and I think you have some idea of his strength of character and forcefulness, Nurse Turner.' Sister sighed. 'He's much too nice a man to miss the good things of life. I hope that Nurse Bond manages to make him see her as a possible partner.'

Jennifer opened the cupboard doors and took out the equipment for the afternoon but she had no idea of what she was doing. She heard his voice again in her mind . . . 'are you pregnant, Nurse?' There now seemed a kind of sadness in the question, as if he had heard it all before and hated to think of a young woman being so careless of her life, her youth and her reputation to let it happen to her. Did he now assume that every girl with brown eyes and fair hair was a tramp? Was that why he looked at her with such scorn and couldn't let an opportunity pass without making her feel uncomfortable or furious? Was he venting his remembered wrath on any girl who reminded him of her?

The afternoon passed somehow, with most of the nurses so busy checking their notes and trying to learn anatomy that they didn't notice that Jennifer did very little, except roll bandages and tidy drawers although it wasn't her turn to do so. Sister glanced at her pale face and wondered if she was pining for that nice young man who came to the tea shop in Epsom. If, as he said, they were engaged to be married then Nurse Turner had kept very quiet about it. Most girls would be bubbling over to tell every person she met about her engagement. Sister walked over to the seat where Jennifer was now checking her own notes against a text book. In a way, it would be a pity if she gave up nursing to get married before she had been at Beatties long enough to really enjoy her work.

Jennifer looked up. 'I was looking up the gall bladder, Sister. Nurse Bond told us about one of the patients on Ward 2.'

'Name, Nurse? We must call every patient by name if we are referring directly to him. Only if you are discussing a particular condition without mentioning any one patient do you call it a case.'

'I think his name was Mr Gunter, Sister. I think that's what Nurse Bond called him.'

Sister pointed out the common bile duct on the diagram and told her something of the function of the liver. 'But you will learn more about the details when you go into Block after your months trial on a ward,' she said.

'That seems ages away . . . if I get that far,' said Jennifer sadly.

'What makes you think you'll be leaving? Don't you like it here? Or is that nice young man of yours pressing for you to get married?' Sister smiled kindly. 'I think you show promise, Nurse. Try to stay for a while, even if you leave before you finish training . . . but it seems a shame.'

'Married? I'm not getting married, Sister. My one ambition has been to train at Beatties and I desperately want to stay.' Sister saw tears very near the surface. 'My one dread is that I shall do something terrible and be thrown out.'

'My dear girl, whatever gave you that idea? We aren't a lot of ogres. You are as good as any nurse I've had in this school, and if your work continues to be as satisfactory, I see no reason why you should have a bad report. After that, as you know, you go to Ward 2 for a month and Sister will write another report. If you pass that, you will change into blue and go to another ward for three months.'

'And if I don't pass the test on Ward 2?' Her hands were trembling. 'Must it be Ward 2, Sister? Couldn't I be the one to go to the other surgical ward?'

'I'm afraid you have to go where you are sent, Nurse. Ward 2 is a very good place to work. They do a great deal of interesting surgery and the patients coming and going so quickly makes the atmosphere cheerful and satisfying.'

'I know, Sister, and I like the thought of a surgical ward, but I don't think they like me there.' She hung her head and spoke in a low voice. 'I've already disgraced myself once there . . . and I dread going near the ward again.'

'What rubbish! I know that you had one bad experience. Sister told me about the sterilised pack, but surely you enjoyed it today? Did something happen to make you uneasy? It isn't like Nurse Bond to bully new nurses. She may be brusque when she's busy, but we all suffer from that occasionally. I can't imagine . . .'

'It wasn't Nurse Bond, Sister. She taught us a lot and was very interesting. She even showed us how to lay up a trolley for a lumbar puncture.'

Sister regarded her thoughtfully. 'And did the cruel Mr Smythe come to do the lumbar puncture?'

'How did you know?' Jennifer was wide eyed.

'It follows,' said Sister dryly. 'Mr Smythe is the surgical registrar on that firm and I believe the lumbar puncture in question was one he had to do on a very ill patient who shows signs of cerebral pressure. It's one he wouldn't leave to a house surgeon to do. Mr Price, the patient, is very fortunate to have someone who was bright enough to spot the symptoms so early so that surgery is possible. Sister told me that Mr Price has gone to a unit in another hospital where he's undergoing brain surgery at this very moment.'

'Do you know every patient in the hospital, Sister?'

'By no means.' Sister laughed. 'But you've already found out how difficult it is for nurses to meet without talking shop and Sister is a friend as well as a colleague. We trained together way back and we like it here.' She frowned. 'But that doesn't explain why you are frightened of our very clever and attractive young man.'

'I'm not afraid of him,' said Jennifer, with more spirit, 'but every time I see him, he makes fun of me and shows that he doesn't have time for inefficient or . . . I mean, he doesn't like me because he's formed an unfortunate and wrong impression of me.'

Sister raised her eyebrows. 'Well, you aren't likely to run into him today. He's gone to assist with Mr Price's operation and I think that Nurse Bond might be meeting him this evening.' She smiled. 'She might thaw him out a little before you have to see him again.'

'Yes, Sister,' said Jennifer, but there was no sense of relief in her heart. Where were they going ... Nurse Bond and Mr Smythe? Off duty, would they relax together, eat together ... make love? She tried to concentrate on her notes.

'You saw him again and he upset you?'

Jennifer looked up, startled. 'Yes, Sister.'

'And he teased you again, I suppose. That man is one of the nicest men, but he delights in teasing new house surgeons and nurses.'

'He doesn't tease, Sister. He dislikes me. I know it and I know that if I have to work in that ward, I'll not pass my month's trial.'

'I think you're being a little hyper-sensitive, Nurse, and you will just have to try to cope with a little teasing. Cheer up. You have a very nice boy friend, or should I say fiancé, with broad shoulders who will be only too pleased to lend them to you for weeping on.'

'He's *not* my fiancé, Sister. I didn't ask him to come here and I am definitely *not* engaged.' Her face was flushed. 'All I want is to be allowed to get on with my career, but if Mr Smythe hates me, I fail to see how I can cope with Ward 2.'

'But your friend told me that he was going to take a fairly badly paid job as a games master just so you could have long holidays together when you marry. I thought it was a very refreshing approach to life. It's good to see a man getting his priorities right.'

Jennifer shook her head helplessly. It was no good

trying to explain. Everyone in this hospital misunderstood the situation. Mr Smythe thought she was unattractive, slovenly in her off-duty dress, sadly lacking in common sense and an easy lay, with the liklihood of being pregnant. Sister saw Nigel, selfish, sadistic Nigel, as a kind of white knight. And even dear Charles, so kind and warm, didn't understand that the last thing she wanted was to form an attachment to any man until she had at least begun her training.

'Cheer up,' said Kate as they left the lecture room. 'You've been in a dream all the afternoon. Come on, snap out of it and let's go to a film in the West End this evening. After the company of Arabella, I feel like a little sophistication, a touch of the idle life and I'd like to smell of something better than disinfectant. We could go to an early show, have something to eat and come back convinced that an outside world still exists.' She saw that Jennifer was hesitating. 'Come on, you've a touch of the nunnery about you that isn't quite healthy. I'm going to soak in a bath, wash my hair and put on some war paint.'

'Right . . . I'll just go down to the lodge to post a letter I forgot to send and I'll see you. You're right, it will be fun.' Jennifer smiled, glad to shake off her depression. She wandered out into the mild air. It would be good to see the trees in St James's Park. I'll take some bread and we can feed the ducks before we go into the cinema, she thought. She posted her letter and turned back to the Nurses' Home. Staff Nurse Bond was coming out, glancing at her watch. She was very smartly dressed, her dark hair gleaming and the expertly applied make-up enhancing her fine colouring.

'Did you hear the bus go?' she called. 'Oh, I wish the hospital was nearer a tube station.'

'Hurry ... there's another that goes up West, Nurse,' said Claud, the porter in the lodge.

Jennifer turned to stare at the graceful figure half running down the drive. Was she on her way to meet Mr Nicholas Smythe?

CHAPTER FIVE

'I'D never have recognised you if you hadn't been with Kate,' said Charles Bird. 'Talk about Cinderella blossoming out over night . . . you look wonderful.' Jennifer blushed as he stared at her, making no attempt to hide his amazed admiration.

'So you think I look awful on duty . . . I left my second head and my wooden leg in the Nurses' Home,' she said lightly.

'No, you look great at any time, but this is really something else. Been to a party?' He frowned, as if suspecting that she might have had too good a time without him.

'We went to St James's and spent so long there as it was such a lovely evening that we were a bit late for a show. Could have gone to a cinema but there was nothing but X certificate horrors and we can see them when they come locally. It was nice just to walk and look at the ducks.'

'Have you had supper?'

'No,' said Jennifer. 'We went into Piccadilly and found it was pretty sordid. Nothing but men with dark eyes and flashing teeth trying to pick us up, and a couple of very pathetic junkies sitting on the kerb waiting for their prescriptions to be ready.' She smiled rather sadly. 'Suddenly, it seemed so much better here, so we caught this bus, were promptly ignored by one Charles Bird who had the cheek to climb on to the top deck and sit behind us, and we thought we might splash out and eat in the bar at the Falcon.

'Can I come too?' He looked unsure of himself. 'You haven't a date?'

'You can have the full benefit of our company and our beauty,' said Kate, 'On one condition.'

'Anything,' he said dramatically.

'We all go Dutch,' said Kate firmly. 'My brother is a student and I know just how hard up you are as a race. It saves a lot of bother if we agree at the outset and stick to it. We all pay our way.'

'Just as well,' said Charles. 'You might get fed better that way. With me it would be half a pint and a sandwich.' He grinned cheerfully. 'I'm glad I met you.'

'Why? Are most of your girl friends expensive?' teased Kate. 'Have they cleaned you out already?'

Dusk was settling over the suburbs as they reached the hospital. Kate and Jennifer went in to freshen up and Charles said he'd meet them by the gate leading to the park next door to Beatties. By the time the girls came out of the gate, the moon had risen, casting shadows along the line of trees, sending shafts of light between the leaves of the limes and making a deep pink and white carpet of the fallen blossom from the ornamental cherry trees. Jennifer looked up at the maiden moon and her heart ached . . . 'On such a night . . .' but what could possibly happen to her on such a night or any other night? With Nigel? No. With Charles? She watched him slip down from the wall on which he sat waiting. He was good-looking, warm-hearted and thoroughly nice. He was a dear, but he was not the man to make her look at the moon and sigh for she knew not what. Would there be such a man? Could any man awaken her and make her forget her wish to give her life to nursing the sick? She had a vision of a face that was half man, half devil, but wholly male.

'About time, too,' said Charles and tucked Jennifer's hand under one arm and Kate's under the other. 'I feel safe to go through the park now,' he said, 'I get scared on my own.'

'Who would attack you?' said Kate.

'I was hoping that one of you might,' he said, but his eyes were for Jennifer. A group of local boys passed by, shouting and making a great show of the beer bottles they carried. 'See you later in casualty,' said Charles softly, when they'd gone on their noisy way. 'It's a wonder that more don't come in to us with all the broken bottles they leave lying around.'

Kate asked him about drugs. 'Those boys we saw . . . do you know much about drugs, Charles?'

'Have they taught you anything yet?' he said.

'Only on Ward 2. Nurse Bond showed us the drug cupboard and the keys that either she or Sister carry all the time they are on duty. It seemed quite a performance,' said Jennifer. 'They had one key for the main drug cupboard and another for a cupboard within the cupboard, where the dangerous drugs are kept. Surely, in hospital, they would be safe in the one cupboard. The nurse in charge, or Sister, is the only one to keep that special key and everything has to be checked and signed for.'

'You've never seen anyone the worse for drugs?' said Charles.

'Only the ones today at close quarters. I wouldn't know what they were taking.'

'We have to learn all the signs and symptoms of the common addictive drugs before we go into casualty for a stint. It's amazing how many come in and say they are in pain just to get a shot. Unless we know about drugs, it would be easy to dole out any amount of stuff without realising the harm we might do,' said Charles.

'But surely, you can tell . . . they look odd, don't they?'

'No, that's the trouble. They look normal and well-dressed very often, and it seems that they become cunning like alcoholics and can lie very convincingly. The last people you would suspect turn out to be bad cases.' He grinned. 'Sister in Cas. is a wonder. She's better than a drug squad dog . . . she can smell out drugs or sense that a person is lying very quickly. She also knows most of the local addicts by sight and alerts us if she suspects anything is wrong.' He laughed. 'In fact, a friend of mine who works in Cas. says that if someone is avoiding Sister, he makes sure that Sister sees whoever it is and either nods or shakes her head.'

'I'm sure I've never met anyone with that problem,' said Jennifer.

'I've met a few . . . sometimes ran across them in my other job,' said Kate.

'Doctors and nurses aren't immune,' said Charles. 'I can imagine an overworked GP taking something to keep him going when called out at night, and night nurses might do the same. It's rare, but it happens,' said Charles. 'But my drug tonight is a club sandwich and a pint of the Falcon's best bitter!'

They went into the bar and found a corner table. Kate went to order food while Charles carried drinks, and Jennifer stayed to keep the table booked as a flood of people followed them, filling the remaining tables. She shrugged out of her jacket, pulling down the sleeves of her silk shirt and making sure it was well anchored in the waist band of her brown velvet trousers. The amber silk was the perfect foil to her golden hair, which curled over her shoulders as if glad of the freedom from the restricting French pleat endured during duty hours. She glanced in a mirror on the wall. Do I really look so different? Nurse Bond said I looked quite a different person with a mask and Charles really did have to stare before he believed it was me on the bus. She smiled. At least Mr Smythe hadn't recognised her as the girl he had bawled out when she was wearing a mask. She tried to find some consolation in her ability to change her appearance, but all she could think was that he hated her with or without a mask.

I wonder what he'd think of me now? Would he know me as the girl who annoyed him . . . the girl who he despised and had accused of being pregnant, or would he see another person again, quite different from either of them? She had the sensation that someone was staring at her and instinctively turned slightly. Mr Smythe was sitting at a side table with Staff Nurse Bond. His face was pale, his eyes glinted with the fire of a sad satyr and his hand stayed poised in mid air, holding the glass of wine he had forgotten completely. His eyes seemed to bore into her own, the distance between the two tables seemed to dwindle and she felt that if she put out a hand, she could touch him. A sensation of awareness of him, as a man . . . as a dominant, demanding being, made her heart flutter like a frightened tiny creature. She took the one refuge left . . . a refuge she hadn't used since she was a child . . . she shook her hair forward and hid her eyes in its long, curling waves.

'Lost a hair grip?' said Kate.

Jennifer flung back her hair, but now she was sitting with her back to Mr Smythe. 'No, thought I'd move round. Anyone mind? I like this view better.'

'I don't mind,' said Charles. 'It brings you closer to me.'

Kate turned round, curious to see who or what Jennifer was avoiding. 'As if you didn't know,' she whispered. 'Your pet demon is with us.'

Charles was happily unaware of any tension and picked up the conversation where he had left it before ordering the food. His voice droned above her head and Jennifer tried to forget the look in the dark eyes that still seemed to be looking at her. He hates me in one kind of dress . . . he despises me in another, and now . . . he looks at me as if he's seen a ghost. There was a mercurial bond of bruised memory that she could not recognise, but which flowed from him to her with sadness. This time he isn't cross, she thought, with growing wonder. There was caring in that intent appraisal.

'Eat up,' said Charles. 'I thought you were hungry.' He started on his second ham roll and looked longingly at the fast cooling club sandwich on Jennifer's plate. 'If you're going anorexic, I'll eat it before it's ruined,' he said. Jennifer cut the sandwich in half and gave him the larger of the two portions. She made a valiant effort to eat the rest. 'It's very good,' said Charles. 'I wish I'd ordered one instead of these rather bready ham rolls.' He was content to be with the two girls, putting no pressures on anyone but just enjoying their company, but he glanced at Jennifer and in his eyes was a growing awareness of her appeal.

'It's getting late,' said Jennifer. 'Drink up, Kate, we have work to do tomorrow.'

Charles stretched. 'I have work to do tonight. I see my boss over there. I'm to accompany him on a night round.' He grinned wryly. 'He works himself into the ground and expects everyone to do the same. I'll go back with you and be there, all bright and intelligent and . . . early. It looks as if he has a rather luscious date, so he might be late.'

As they passed the table where Mr Nicholas Smythe and Nurse Bond sat, Jennifer glanced down at the dark head. He was listening to his companion, with an intent absorption in what she was saying. 'I'm glad we've decided,' said Nurse Bond. 'Shall I definitely fix a date?' She was looking at him with large dark eyes that said very plainly, 'I love you' and Jennifer forced herself to walk naturally away, without a backward glance. She had not seen his eyes but, surely, her face was enough. To fix a date might mean anything . . . a meeting, a lecture . . . a holiday or . . . a wedding.

The park was bathed in moonlight, wonderful, pale and heartless moonlight. It was a place filled with a magic it never experienced during the day

. . . a place where anything could happen, lovers could meet, vows be exchanged, and it was where she knew Mr Smythe would take Nurse Bond on the way home. 'What's her first name?' said Jennifer.

'Whose?'

'Nurse Bond, of course,' she said, as if she must be in all their thoughts.

'Victoria,' said Charles, 'and she prefers that to any abbreviation . . . not that humble mortals like me are asked to use that name. She reserves it for Old Nick and his ilk.'

Kate watched her friend as they said goodnight to Charles. She was pale and withdrawn and hardly aware that he had left them. 'Cheer up . . . he didn't bite you, did he? Seemed to be rather interested in a melancholy way, I thought. What really gives between you and him?'

'Charles?'

'No, you know very well who I mean . . . Nicholas Smythe.'

'I don't even know the man,' said Jennifer.

'He'll know you again . . . even in that disguise,' said Kate.

'It's only that he thinks he's seen me somewhere and can't place me,' said Jennifer. She tried to laugh. 'Even Charles didn't know me on the bus. I have at least three personalities . . . didn't you know?'

'Coffee?' said Kate. 'I don't feel like going to bed yet. I didn't have any in the Falcon and now I'm thirsty.' She glanced anxiously at Jennifer. 'Come on, you look as if you could do with some. Are you sure you are all right?'

'Fine,' said Jennifer, shaking back her hair and

mentally shaking away her sudden depression. 'I've some freshly ground coffee in my room. It wouldn't take long to make it in a jug.'

'Pity Charles couldn't have joined us. It's stupid refusing to let medical students into the Home after eleven. If we wanted a tumble it doesn't *have* to be after ten at night!'

'Sister said it was because they make too much noise and wake everyone who is trying to sleep.'

Kate put the kettle on to boil and rooted in the fridge for milk. Then she decided that, as a very junior nurse, it might seem presumptuous to take the last half pint and dashed off to her room to get some powdered milk and coffee whitener. I hope Jen doesn't object to it in her good coffee, she thought.

'Kate?' Jennifer turned at the sound behind her in the kitchen. She had glanced in the sitting room while the coffee was brewing and wondered where her friend had gone, then went back to the coffee making, wondering if she dared eat some biscuits, suddenly hungry and aware that she had wasted the food in the Falcon. How could a man like Nicholas Smythe rob her of her appetite? Even when she had been very upset with Nigel she had never been like this and, tonight, Mr Smythe had no cause for anger at anything she did. She heard voices in the sitting room and called 'Kate?' She put two mugs on a tray and took biscuits from her tin. 'Want any biscuits?' she called.

'Is that *real* coffee?' Nurse Bond stood in the doorway, smiling. She looked at Jennifer as if she didn't know who she was. 'Are you working at Beatties?' she said, then gasped. 'You're Nurse Turner.'

'Sorry I kept you,' said Kate. 'Oh, sorry, Nurse Bond. I brought some of this stuff. It's not bad in coffee. Would you like some?' Kate seemed to be on the point of throwing a fit. She had her back to Nurse Bond and her eyes rolled as if she wanted Jennifer to look behind her. 'How many cups, Nurse Bond?' said Kate with unnecessary emphasis. 'Do you take sugar? Let me bring it in to you,' she babbled.

'It's quite all right, Nurse, we'll come in here,' said Bond. Jennifer raised her eyebrows and Kate nodded. A moment later, a familiar tall figure stood leaning against the draining board, smiling at Kate. Jennifer edged towards the door away from him, her face shrouded by her long hair. She reached the door and fled, unable to face the sardonic smile, the lazy humour and the incredibly potent magnetism of the man who disliked her so much.

'Brought you some of *your* coffee,' said Kate, five minutes later. 'Who's a little coward, then?' She chuckled. 'No wonder Charles calls you Mouse. I can't think what you have to be scared about. Mr Smythe is really very amusing, very charming and . . . very kind.' She looked at the girl sitting on the bed. 'Yes, very kind. He wanted to come up to make sure you were all right. He saw you in the Falcon and caught a glimpse of you in the kitchen and when I made the excuse that you had a headache, he wanted to check.'

'He's not coming up here?'

'Relax . . . he doesn't know who you are or where you fit into Beatties. That hair of yours really does strange things to your appearance. But he was genuinely concerned, which doesn't quite fit the picture you have of him as the unfeeling brute who insults you at every turn.' Kate smiled. 'If Nurse Bond wasn't so obviously in charge of our resident god Pan, I'd have a try for him myself. He's the most vital piece of man I've seen in months.'

Jennifer sipped the coffee. 'Thanks Kate. I'm all right, but I couldn't face him tonight. It would have spoiled what had been a very good evening.'

'So you enjoyed being with Charles? You could do a lot worse, Jen. He's alright.'

'Stop trying to pair me off. Tomorrow, I have my hair cut very short, shaved if necessary, and I become a nun,' laughed Jennifer. 'Then, even Charles and Nigel will turn away from me. Shall I take the mugs back?'

'Better not, in case you run into the bogy man,' teased Kate. 'I have to go down again to pick up my powdered milk. I thought I saw Roberta Marne come in. She might like some coffee, if those greedy love birds have left any. My, my, Nurse Bond looks as if she could eat him whole.'

'And Mr Smythe?'

Kate looked serious. 'I don't know. He treats her as if he's fond of her, but I don't sense any real passion there. When that man loses his heart, if he hasn't already done so, then meteors will fall, lightning flash and all the world will know.' Jennifer shivered. 'You aren't sickening for something are you?' said Kate.

'No, of course not. Take the mugs and I'll put away my coffee. It was very good, I thought.'

'And Mr Smythe thought so, too. Asked me to

thank you,' said Kate as she went out of the room.

Jennifer sat in the chair, staring at the wall. He thought she was inefficient, immoral, pregnant and very unattractive . . . but at least he admitted that she made good coffee. Which one is me? The nurse with hair scraped back who puts fingers into unsterile packs? The girl who mixes up her boy friends or the young woman he saw in the Falcon and couldn't place in his memory? Well, I suppose it's good to know he approves of something.

'Jen . . . can you come?' Kate's anxious face showed round the door. Jennifer zipped up the front of her blue velvet dressing gown and followed her. She saw Kate disappear into the end room by the stairs. 'What do you think?' said Kate. Roberta Marne lay·on the bed in her room. Her coat was undone and her handbag gaped wide. The girl's face was pale and slightly moist, her eyes bright but strange. She sighed and tried to focus her gaze on Jennifer but gave up the effort and sank back, smiling.

'Is she drunk?' whispered Jennifer. 'How did she get back if she was in this state?'

'I think it was closer to home,' said Kate. From the open handbag, she took a bottle of pills.

'They're from Ward 3. Look at the label. They're Pentobarbitone tablets. That's a barbiturate, I think,' said Jennifer. 'Aren't they habit forming?'

Kate looked grave. 'I think she took these from the ward when she was there for the day, learning about the drug cupboards. If they had been prescribed, the bottle would have her name on it.' She looked down at the young woman on the bed. By now, Roberta was breathing heavily and was in a deep sleep, fully dressed.

'What can we do? If anyone finds out, she'll have to leave. I know that one of the rules says no nurse may take any drug that has not been prescribed by the medical officer in charge. Even a couple of aspirins have to be noted if a sister gives them to a nurse in training for a headache on duty.'

'The important question is . . . has she taken much and has she taken them before tonight?' said Kate. 'I know people who take mild drugs as a matter of course. A sub-editor I know makes a joke of taking "uppers" and "downers" and sometimes getting mixed up when he's under stress.' She looked at Roberta. 'Well, this is a "downer" for sure.' She bent forward. 'Ah . . . she's had at least one brandy, which would make the effect worse. I wonder . . .'

'Can you think of a way we can help without letting her have any more? It would be a pity if she had to leave Beatties before she even starts her training.'

'I'd like to give her a chance,' said Kate, 'But we'll have to wait until she wakes up and make sure that this is the first time.' She took the bottle and put it in her own pocket. 'We can't do anything now. I'll set my alarm half an hour earlier than usual and we'll talk in the morning.'

'How can we get them back to the ward?' said Jennifer. 'I'm going to Ward 3 tomorrow with some special dressing packs that Sister made for them there. One of the consultants is very fussy and likes very small amounts of dressings which he can use and discard and not use twice. As usual, there is at least one sister who spoils him and makes them specially ... this time, it's our Sister Jones!' She frowned. 'Do you think I could put the bottle back?'

'Risky,' said Kate, 'but you could keep it in your pocket and then drop them in the clinical room if you find it impossible. They'll never know who left them and although they might make a fuss, no one in particular could be blamed.'

Kate closed the door softly as they left Roberta's room and put out her light. 'Better get to bed if we're to be up very early,' she said. 'Oh, I'd better give you these in case I forget in the morning.' She held out the bottle of barbiturates as they stood under the landing light.

'And what do you think you two are doing?' The cold voice of Nurse Bond cut the silence of the sleeping corridor. Kate gasped and thrust the bottle back into her bag. 'Give me that bottle at once.' Nurse Bond took the bottle from Kate's nervous grasp and examined the label. She looked up at the two scared faces. 'This is serious. Who took this from Ward 3?' The two girls remained silent. 'Very well, if you refuse to tell me, I have no alternative. I shall report the matter to the sister on Ward 3 and your own sister tutor in the morning.' She turned away and walked up to the next landing where she had her room on the upper corridor.

'At least she was alone,' said Jennifer. 'Nurse Bond is bad enough but I should have died on the spot if Mr Smythe was with her. He would add one more sin to my list ... in his eyes I really would be less than the dust if he thought I took drugs!'

'Better get to bed,' said Kate. 'I have a feeling

that a balloon is about to burst . . . in my head. I don't think we can shield Roberta now. In a way, I'm glad. She had no right to take them and she might need more specialised help than she can expect from us. Goodnight . . . and cheer up, we'll explain in the morning.'

As Jennifer went into her room, she wondered why Nurse Bond had seemed . . . almost pleased that she was in trouble. It had been at her she had looked, even though Kate was the one who had the drug bottle in her hand. It seemed she wanted Jennifer to be blamed, more than Kate. In her eyes there had been a glimpse of something like triumph. She hates me, thought Jennifer, with a shiver. She has no cause . . . although she was annoyed to think Mr Smythe spoke to me. It's ridiculous, she thought. He doesn't like me and she seemed to have his full attention . . . his devotion, in the Falcon.

CHAPTER SIX

THE cap pin was digging into her scalp but Jennifer dared do nothing about it. Her hair was scraped back as tightly as possible, her uniform was spotless and her tights were new. Both she and Kate had appeared on duty as if about to face a rigid inspection and Sister Jones had commented on their smart appearance. If you only knew why we made the extra effort, you wouldn't smile so indulgently, she thought glumly.

Kate idly splashed water in the jug, stirring it with the enema tube. She looked at Arabella as if she was quite her most unfavourite person, sighed and folded back the bed clothes. 'If she leaks like she did the last time, I give in. I shall warn every real patient I meet that I give only leaky enemas and that most of the stuff I inject never returns. Arabella must be water-logged!' she said.

'How can you be so bright?' said Jennifer. 'I haven't seen Roberta this morning . . . has she been told to stay away?'

'I don't see why. We're the only ones who know about last night. Oh . . . look out . . . trouble.'

Sister Jones came towards them, her face set in a disapproving and slightly incredulous expression. 'Have you taken the packs to Ward 3 as I asked, Nurse Turner? I did say they must be there first thing this morning, before the ward round. I'm surprised at you. I began to feel that I could rely on you.'

'I wasn't sure if you had finished them, Sister. Yesterday, you said you'd tell me when they were complete and you said nothing when I went off duty.'

Sister's face cleared. 'I'm sorry. It was my fault, but I wish you'd asked. It slipped my mind and I remember now that I didn't tell you. Take them now, and hurry. Nurse Bond rang just now to remind me about the packs.' She smiled. 'She's very good. I was talking to her about them and she mentioned you. When I said I had told you to take them to Ward 3, she laughed and hoped you weren't as scared there as you had been on her ward. Nice of her to think I might need a reminder; when Ward 3 is really nothing to do with her; but she is very efficient.'

Jennifer took the bundle and left the lecture room. Kate frowned and spilled water on the bed cover but had no time to speak to Jennifer before she left. Ward 3 was easy to find as it was on the ground floor near the main corridor. Jennifer hovered at the entrance, peeping through the round window in the wooden outer door. She could see a nurse beyond the inner glass doors and went into the clinical room. The room was similar in size and shape to all the other clinical rooms in the main wards of Beatties, but this one had rather more bottles of lotions and pots of unguents as it was the ward where skin diseases were treated. Soiled dressings smelled of antiseptics and surgical spirit and the trolley towels lacked the brightness of towels in other wards. It's as

99

if they wash in Brand X thought Jennifer, but knew that it was difficult to remove all traces of the dyes used in some treatments.

A patient came into the room. He wore a hospital dressing-gown stained with gentian violet and his head was bandaged neatly, the stark white covering showing the underlying edge of violet in contrast. He emptied a dish of swabs into the bin and put the metal dish in the sink. 'I can do most of it, now,' he said with pride. 'They just do my head.' He went back into the ward, calling the nurse and telling her that one of the nurses from up the road was waiting in the clinical room, with all the confidence of a long term patient who thinks he knows everything.

Jennifer gulped. I hate to think if much of him is covered with that awful dye, she thought. She turned to see the ward sister standing there. 'I brought the packs, Sister,' said Jennifer. 'I'm sorry they are late but there was a slight misunderstanding.' She stared at the bottle in Sister's hand and recognised it as the bottle of pentobarbicane they had discovered in Roberta Marne's room.

Sister Coates looked stern. 'Well, Nurse? What have you to say about this? Nurse Bond told me that you would be bringing the packs, so I decided to do nothing until I saw you and gave you a chance to explain. Sit down and look up at the light.'

'But Sister . . .'

'Do as I say, Nurse. I want to decide for myself if you are just foolish and experimental or . . . dependent. In either case, the result will be the same when the medical superintendent and Matron hear about this. You do realise that under no circumstances can a nurse who takes drugs be a fit person to work at the Princess Beatrice Hospital?'

Jennifer sank on to the metal chair and found that her hands were shaking. Sister saw them too and clucked her disapproval. She raised the right eyelid of the trembling girl and then the left. She grunted. 'But Sister . . . I can explain,' began Jennifer desperately. Sister quelled her with a glance, and carefully felt for her pulse. She looked puzzled. Jennifer stood up, her courage returning. 'Sister . . . you must listen. It isn't fair to accuse me without proof.'

'I have the word of a senior staff nurse that she found you in possession of this bottle of pentobarbicane in the Nurses' Home late at night. Nurse Bond is efficient, loyal and hardworking. She is also completely truthful. Give me one reason why I should not believe her?'

'I can give you a reason. I didn't touch them . . . I didn't even touch the bottle!' She recalled the fact that it was Kate who held the bottle until Nurse Bond took it from her. Kate was certainly holding it out for Jennifer to take from her, but she had made no physical contact with the bottle.

Sister hesitated, slightly un-nerved by the clear eyes that flashed angrily and . . . honestly? The anger she could dismiss as guilt but there was some instinct that told her this young woman was not a drug taker. 'Do you deny that you have seen this bottle at some time before this morning?'

'I don't deny it, Sister.'

'And did you see it in the Nurses' Home last night?'

'Yes, Sister.'

'Well, you admit that much. It's a start. I haven't all day to spend on one very junior nurse, so I'd be very much obliged if you'd tell me the rest. I have only your word against that of Nurse Bond, who I know and trust, and you have admitted seeing the bottle last night. Why not make a clean breast of it, Nurse. If you took it for a joke, for any reason other than to take the drug, I'm sure that you will have a fair hearing and perhaps not be expelled from Beatties.'

'Expelled? Oh, no, Sister . . . not that. I swear I . . .'

'Sister? Dr Spencer is waiting in your office. He's been there for ten minutes and is getting impatient,' said the staff nurse. She glanced curiously at the pale face and tear-filled eyes.

'I'll be along,' said Sister sharply, discouraging comment. The door closed again. 'Now, listen to me, Nurse. I want no scandal attached to my ward, so I forbid you to mention this to anyone not involved. Is that understood?' She flushed. 'As Nurse Bond pointed out, the fewer people concerned with this, the better. I don't want the whole hospital buzzing with the fact that Ward 3 is incapable of looking after its drugs.' She opened the door. 'Come to my room in the Nurses' Home after duty tonight. I shall be out until nine-thirty and will see you then.'

Jennifer stared after her, her mind confused. One minute she was threatening instant dismissal and the next, she seemed about to enter a covering-up agreement with Nurse Bond.

She walked slowly back to the school, in time to meet the rest of the nurses in the small dining room where they were devouring bread and dripping and coffee. 'Special treat today,' said the catering student. 'Not often we have real dripping. I hadn't eaten it before I began my course and I doubt whether you'll eat anything like it when you begin training.' She sprinkled salt on a slice of bread liberally covered with beef dripping and handed it to Jennifer, who promptly turned even paler and fled to the lavatory where she was very sick.

'Are you all right?' Kate's anxious voice came through the partition. Jennifer opened the door and came out. 'Here, rinse with this. Betty found some soda water. It's good after . . . that.'

'Thanks.' Jennifer washed her mouth out and spat. She drank some soda water slowly and felt better. 'I'm all right,' she said. 'I had a shock, but I can't tell you now.'

'Nurse Turner?' Sister Jones looked anxious. 'What caused that? Did you eat out last night? How do you feel? You looked fine this morning . . . or, come to think of it, you looked a bit odd when I sent you with the packs to Ward 3. You managed to do that, safely?' she added anxiously.

'Yes, Sister . . . it's just that dripping isn't my idea of a treat.'

'Can't think why,' said Sister Jones briskly, wiping her fingers on a piece of tissue. 'Delicious. Only the gall bladder sufferers and the pregnant refuse such luxury,' she said, trying to make Jennifer smile, then gazed with a comical expression of alarm as Jennifer burst into tears. 'Well . . . what did I say?'

'I'm not pregnant . . . I'm not, I'm not!'

'All right . . . you're not pregnant . . . no need to

carry on like that, Nurse. I think you are unwell. Go to your room and lie down. Nurse Minter . . . go with her and make her go to bed. Report back to me and I'll see her at lunch time.' Silly girls . . . I suppose she had a tiff with that nice young man of hers . . . she was very eager to convince me that she isn't pregnant. I wonder . . . she thought.

'What was all that about?' said Kate as they walked slowly towards the hospital. 'I ate the same as you yesterday. I'm fine. I even had two slices of bread and dripping. It took me back to my grannie's place in Wales. It's delicious.'

'Don't.' Jennifer shuddered. 'I still feel a bit fragile. Do you mind not talking about that?'

'If it's not stomach . . . it's in the mind . . . tell Auntie Kate.'

'I can't . . . she told me not to say anything.'

'Who did? Sister Jones?'

'No, the sister on Ward 3.'

'It's about the drugs! So Nurse Bond did tell her?' She led Jennifer up the stairs to her room. 'Come on, I'm in this too, you know. Why wasn't anything said to me?'

'Oh, Kate. I began to feel all alone.' Jennifer told her what had happened when she saw the sister.

'But that's screwy! Sister Jones doesn't know, that's obvious. Nurse Bond said she intended telling her this morning, but all was sweetness and light. I don't get it. Did Sister what's-it on Ward 3 mention me?' Jennifer sank back on the bed and shook her head. 'And we haven't split on Roberta yet. Why would Nurse Bond point the finger on you and not me? I was the one with the wretched bottle in my hand, not you.'

'I told Sister that I hadn't even touched the bottle, but she said that she had Nurse Bond's word for it, and she believed her.'

'Wait a minute. I'm going along to Roberta's room. She isn't on duty and Sister doesn't seem to have missed her.'

Jennifer closed her eyes. Her head swam with a blurred mixture of thoughts, questions she couldn't answer and fears that, somehow, she would have to leave Beatties, the hospital she knew she would love doing her training in. Why me? Why not Kate? It would be all right when they told what had really happened, but it was hurtful to be accused of something so foreign to her nature. Like the other accusation ... he thought I was pregnant, she recalled. Sister must think so too, now I've taken so much time denying it ... 'methinks the lady doth protest too much' ... was often true.

'She's gone ... cases, clothes, everything. She's done a bunk!'

Jennifer forgot her headache and went after Kate. The room was neat and bare. 'Are you sure this was the room?' She looked at the small name ticket on the door. Nurse Roberta Marne, it said. 'But she loves it here ... she said that Beatties was a revelation after that psychiatric hospital where she worked ... or one of them. We never did find out exactly where, did we?'

Kate frowned. 'I'd better go back and tell Sister. After all, she's in charge of us and will know what to do. I'll tell her everything that happened, including your little session today.'

'No, you can't do that. Sister forbade me to discuss it with anyone not involved.'

'Well, I'm involved and you've told me and I've made no such promise,' said Kate firmly. 'I also want to know what Nurse Bond is doing. I think she had a very good reason for making sure it was you who took the packs to Ward 3 and saw the sister. She has a grudge against you, Jen, and I mean to find out what it is.'

'But I've done nothing to make her want to hurt me. She has a case that she might think needs investigation, after finding us with the tablets, but I can't think why she left you out! She surely isn't still cross about the telling off she had for letting me help her in the ward? That's over and she seemed quite pleasant after it. I haven't seen her since . . . except the time we had coffee after going to the Falcon with Charles. She *did* seem surprised to find I looked different in off duty clothes . . . but that's all.'

'You remember who she was with?' Kate glanced at Jennifer slyly. 'Your favourite demon. Perhaps he showed a passing interest in you and she was narked as she considers him to be her property.'

'Rubbish,' said Jennifer, colour flooding her face. 'You've a very devious mind. It's all that advertising copy! Go and tell Sister I'm O.K. and I'll come over to see her before lunch.' She called Kate as she left. 'I suppose someone knows about Roberta? That she's gone?'

'I'll ask Sister if Roberta's off sick. That should start something.'

'Do you realise, Kate, that if Roberta doesn't come back and admit that she took the bottle of tablets, it's our word against Nurse Bond and, from what I've heard, it's weighed very much in her favour.'

'Don't worry, I won't let the nasty cat get you, little mouse.' Kate laughed, but it was a false sound, as if she had doubts about her own ability to smooth out the problem.

Jennifer showered and brushed her hair. The long firm strokes of the hair brush soothed and comforted and she began to think rationally. Her stomach ceased to feel queasy and her head was clear again. She put her hair up skilfully, smoothing the glossy roll into shape almost without thinking what she was doing. It was all a part of the uniform now, to be put on neatly and quickly. She knew that everything that had been awkward and time consuming, like doing her hair for duty, fixing the belt by the clipped buckle and pinning her apron, had become as effortless and routine as cleaning her teeth. The work in the school was now easy and the procedures taught there were being absorbed, ready to use to good purpose when real human beings needed her attention.

If I leave Beatties, it will all be wasted, she thought, unless another hospital would take a girl dismissed from one of the best for possession of hospital drugs. She made a great effort to ignore the possibilities, but they were still in her mind as she went back to the school, physically better, but with nerves jangling. Mr Smythe dislikes every aspect of me, Nurse Bond hates me for something and it will soon be rumoured that I was sent off duty because I was sick . . . in the morning, she thought. I wonder if I shall laugh at all this sometime in the future? But she was far from laughter as she opened the door to the lecture room.

'You look much better, Nurse Turner,' said Sister. She smiled a trifle bleakly and Jennifer knew that Kate had talked to her. 'Wait in my office and I'll be with you in five minutes. Time to pack up, Nurses,' she said briskly, and began to tidy her notes. Jennifer sat on the broad window seat of what had been the morning room when Grey Stones was a private house. The ornamental cherry trees were softly leaved, the sun filtering through on to the blossom-covered grass. It must have been a good home . . . a pleasant place to live in, and I may have to leave soon. She turned to the door as it opened, expecting to see Sister Jones. She gasped.

The sunlight made a shaft of gold through the window which found an echo in the gold lights in the girl's hair. Her wide eyes which held deep sadness made her look like a pale Victorian girl in a decline for love or consumption, although the gleam of perfect basic health belied this. The cool blue dress, on which her hands lay passively, added to the virginal look and Nicholas Smythe stared. Was this the girl in the grubby jeans who had fainted after the disco? He recalled the tendrils of escaping hair that softened the frame of severity as he held her in his arms to take her into the Nurses' Home. Ridiculous, he thought. For a moment, he had an almost overwhelming desire to put out a hand and free the bright locks from the confining cap. 'Hello,' he said. 'What have you done this time?'

It was just something to say . . . something to bring

a note of relief to the tension he sensed between them. Nothing that could make a girl look so distressed, surely, unless she *had* done something of which she was ashamed? He saw the huge eyes glisten with unshed tears, the high colour tinging the pale cheeks and the tremendous effort she made to keep her emotions under control. 'I've done nothing,' she said, in a low voice, 'But it's no use saying it. You think I'm guilty, too, don't you? I suppose it will be all over the hospital before I've been given a chance to explain. I can do nothing right in this place . . . you hate me, the sisters think I'm a liar and Nurse Bond is believed without any proof. I should never have come here,' she said bitterly.

She bent her head as if in submission and in his brain a memory stirred. He had seen a head bent like that, but the hair was long and heavy and almost concealed the girl's face. The memory was from another time, another place, but he had been reminded last night when the girl with long golden hair had sat in the Falcon, a girl like this . . . but with hair tumbling over her shoulders, and a shirt of amber silk, not a stiff little dress of pale blue. Why should this girl bring back painful memories? Why the girl in the Falcon? 'Were you in the Falcon last night?' he said.

She started. 'Yes.' The deep brown eyes were expressionless and she looked away again. So he recognised her as the girl with long hair . . . how long before he knew her as the girl in the mask who was such an idiot?

'You look different today and you are very upset.

I saw you with the student who took you to the disco, and didn't recognise you at first.' He smiled. 'What's wrong? You seem to have a persecution complex. Very sensitive? Ill, or bad conscience?'

'My conscience is quite clear, thank you,' she said with dignity.

'Then you must be ill,' he said in a business-like voice. 'Is that why you are in here waiting for Sister? I came over for some notes I mislaid and she asked me to stay as she wanted my advice . . . about you?'

'I'm not ill.' He advanced towards her and firmly took her hand. The firm, warm fingers found her beating pulse and the dark eyes looked gravely and professionally into hers. He held her wrist for a full minute, not checking the rate with his watch, but just regarding her with a puzzled expression. 'I'm not ill,' she repeated, trying to draw away. His nearness was too much to bear. The touch of his hand offered a help she knew he would never give her, the clean scent of after shave and surgical echoes of antiseptics made her realise that he was being wholly professional, taking note of signs and symptoms of any nervous reaction she might show. But it was he who gave her the symptoms, made her desperately try to conceal the signs that she was moved by his presence, aware of him as she had never been aware of another living soul.

She cast down her gaze, knowing that in her eyes he would see something that the text books ignored. I want him . . . more than I've wanted anything in my life, she thought. I know it's only a physical reaction when I'm at a low ebb . . . I know I shall forget as soon as he has gone . . . but please . . . please don't look at me with those magnetic eyes . . . hold my hand in that warm, human grasp when I know that you could never want me in a thousand years.

'Ah, there you are, Mr Smythe. Sorry if I kept you waiting. Nurse Turner was a bit off-colour this morning and I didn't think it worth sending her off sick, so she went to bed for an hour and now seems all right. I think perhaps something is worrying her.'

'I've taken her pulse and she seems fine except for a slight nerviness. Perhaps a couple of tablets might be advisable. These girls have a lot to do when they come here and some can't cope at first. Give her time and I'm sure she'll be as good as new.' He smiled at Sister Jones. I wish they wouldn't treat me as if I wasn't here, thought Jennifer. She coughed loudly.

'A cough? Perhaps you are in for a virus infection,' said Sister.

The dark brown eyes softened. 'I'm afraid we were guilty of the terrible sin of ignoring the patient and talking over her head, Sister,' said Mr Smythe.

'Silly girl,' said Sister. She looked embarrassed. 'I think there is something more . . . why not tell us, Nurse?'

'Has Nurse Minter spoken to you, Sister?'

'She has indeed,' said Sister grimly. 'She is your friend, I know, and wants to help you, but I have to sort out the truth and I don't know where to begin.' She looked troubled. 'You see, Mr Smythe, one of the staff nurses says that she found Nurse Turner with a bottle of barbiturates that belonged to Ward 3. She had them at night, in the Nurses' Home.'

'It isn't true,' said Jennifer. 'I haven't touched

them. I told Sister on Ward 3 and she said she was going to contact you, but I imagine she hasn't had time to see you.'

'She telephoned,' said Sister. 'She said that you admitted seeing the drugs.'

'And did she say that she didn't want it all over the hospital in case everyone had the idea that Ward 3 couldn't look after its own drugs?'

'Don't be impertinent, Nurse. She wants to keep it to as few people as possible in case you have an innocent explanation.'

'That's what Nurse Bond suggested to her,' said Jennifer in a low voice. 'Nurse Bond knows very well that I haven't taken any drugs. Ask Nurse Minter, Sister, if you don't believe me.'

'Nurse Minter is your friend, Nurse. She was not mentioned by either Sister or Nurse Bond, so I can only assume that she is trying to protect you.'

'Is this true?' The dark eyes seemed to be lit with a fire of sadness. He's not angry, only sorry, thought Jennifer.

'I have taken no drugs,' she said simply. 'Nurse Bond saw us in the Nurses' Home. Nurse Minter was holding a bottle of tablets that we found in Nurse Marne's room and we were wondering what to do with them. We saw the label and suspected that they were barbiturates, and Nurse Marne was in no fit state to tell us where she found them.'

'Why didn't you tell Nurse Bond? She never mentioned Nurse Marne as having anything to do with this.' Sister looked confused. 'Nurse Minter said that Nurse Marne had gone, taken all her belongings. When did she discover that? I haven't seen Nurse

Marne as she telephoned when I came on duty saying she had a stomach upset and wouldn't be on duty. I thought that you might have eaten the same food when you were sick this morning, Nurse.'

'You were sick?' The dark eyes glinted. 'Are you quite sure you are all right, Nurse,' he said. 'Shall I make an appointment for you to see the gynaecologist?' The warmth had died and he was as distant as he had ever been, his concern tinged with slight distaste.

'No . . . No . . . how many more times have I to say it? I am not pregnant . . . I have never been pregnant and from what I see of the average man, I hope I shall never be pregnant!' Jennifer glared at the one who thought so little of her.

He glanced at his watch. 'Well, all this is fascinating, Sister, but I have work to do.' He looked coldly at Jennifer. 'Even if she has taken no drugs, I suggest a mild tranquillizer, Sister.' He wrote swiftly on a prescription pad.

Sister took it and thanked him. 'I think I shall do nothing until I have talked to Nurse Bond,' she said.

'Yes . . . I think we shall have the truth from her,' he said, and strode from the room.

'But Sister, Nurse Marne was asleep. She was fully clothed and her eyes looked very peculiar. Nurse Minter said she had seen the look before and thought she had taken some of the tablets and then some brandy.'

Sister Jones straightened the bow under her chin. 'Unfortunately, we have no proof of that unless Nurse Marne comes back . . . if she comes back.'

CHAPTER SEVEN

'I'LL have to go back,' said Jennifer. 'I'm sorry, Charles, but I have to see Sister Coates at nine-thirty and I haven't much time,' She twisted her hair between trembling fingers.

'What gives, little mouse?' he said gently. 'I thought that coming here for a quick drink would brighten you up, but you seem much worse. Is it something I said?' He grinned cheerfully. 'Buck up, we all have exams and nobody likes them. You will be fine.' He stood and pushed back his chair. The lounge at the Falcon was filling up and the atmosphere was friendly and good. 'Sure you can't stay? All right, I'll see you back to the hospital.'

'There's really no need, Charles.'

'And have you ravished in the park or accosted in the road?'

She smiled faintly. 'No one in his right mind would do either. I must look a mess.'

'Never,' he said. 'A bit pale round the gills, but pale is beautiful,' he added lightly. She followed him out into the warm evening. Dear Charles, she thought. Don't fall in love with me. Please don't be hurt. Her own bruised spirit lent her an added sensitivity, telling her that he was already half in love with her. I could never love you, she thought, as they walked back to Beatties. The fire in a pair of dark eyes had consumed her own emotions, leaving her spent and empty, but aware that his love was the only one she wanted. The love of a firm, strong and attractive man who had nothing but dislike for her. He despises me, accepts what Nurse Bond says about me and is probably almost engaged to her.

At the entrance to the Home, Charles bent and kissed her on the cheek. 'Now, promise me you won't work half into the night. No exam is worth it, you know.'

'I promise,' she said, and impulsively raised her face to kiss him. 'You're a dear,' she said.

'I love you too,' he said, trying to keep it light. She broke away, smiling. The door was open and a tall figure stood by the half-table inside. She drew in her breath sharply. He had seen the kiss, heard the tender interchange of goodbyes and she must pass him to go to Sister Coates.

'Ah, there you are.' Jennifer stared at Mr Smythe in horror. He was waiting for her. 'Sister Coates will not be seeing you, Nurse. She has been slightly indisposed this evening.' His voice was cool, his eyes gave away nothing. 'I am here to deal with this in my own way. As I am the only doctor who knows about the episode, I offered . . . no, insisted that as a completely neutral observer, I would be fit to sort out the trouble.'

'Neutral?' Jennifer reddened, angrily. 'You are more involved than Sister Coates. You and Nurse Bond are . . .'

'We are what?'

She looked at the set face and looked away. 'I'm sorry . . . I believed that you and Nurse Bond had something going . . . I mean that you and she were good friends and so you would take her word against mine.'

'I think we should talk quietly,' he said. 'Shall it be here or in the garden? Or would you like to walk in the park?'

She stared. He sounded almost friendly. 'I don't care where it is,' she said, in a low voice. 'Just get it over.'

'The park, then, I think,' he said smoothly. He led her by the arm, helpless and unprotesting, along the paved way to the gate and into the Victorian park. The sound of traffic magically faded, muffled by the tall trees, thick shrubs and the high warm brick wall that separated the park from the dull grey streets outside. He went to a high arch of stone in which was a curved seat and smiled politely at her. 'Will this do? It has a good view of the old fountain, the magnolias and the masterpiece of Victorian architecture over there.' He pointed to the wrought iron roof of the public lavatories. 'Very fine,' he said. 'A friend of mine takes photographs of them to keep a record before they are all gone.'

She sat beside him and glanced up into his face. He was trying to put her at her ease! What had Victorian loos to do with the matter in hand? Was he building up her self confidence only to shatter it by telling her she was finished as far as Beatties was concerned? 'And I suppose you brought your camera?' she said, sarcastically. Even to Jennifer, her voice sounded shrewish, but she knew that she was likely to give away her true feelings at any moment.

'You don't share the enthusiasm? Pity,' he said. He gazed into the growing dusk, the warm air was soft and the park fragrant. Jennifer took a deep breath to keep her self control. Why was he torturing her?

'Well, what have you to say? I suppose you and Nurse Bond and Sister Coates have it all wrapped up without paying any attention to what I might have done or not have done.'

'Yes, it's all settled.' He smiled. 'To tell you the truth, Sister Coates was too embarrassed to speak to you. She asked me to apologise for her. I had a word with Nurse Bond, who says that you misunderstood her. She says that she wanted you to explain how the bottle came to be in the Nurses' Home and didn't mean you any harm. She knows so little about the new nurses that she muddled your names. Nurse Minter was the one who held the drugs . . . as you said to Sister, so Nurse Minter was the one to be in possession of them.'

'But that means you believe Kate takes drugs?' She rounded on him. 'How mean can that woman get. She has no proof and she knows very well we were only wondering what to do for the best.'

'To get the drugs back, perhaps?'

'Yes . . . no . . . to try to get Roberta Marne out of trouble.' She raised sad eyes to him. 'But Roberta's gone. Did you know? Without her, we have no proof. Please say that Kate will not be blamed. She's as innocent as I am.'

'Such innocent eyes . . . beautiful eyes,' he said softly. 'But do they tell the truth? I have known eyes as beautiful that told dangerous lies.' He took her chin in his hand and gazed down at her. Her lips trembled as he kissed them softly, once, then drew away as if coming out of a dream. 'Kate Minter backs up your story and you do the same for her but, as you say, until we find Nurse Marne, there is no proof.' His tone was brisk again and Jennifer could hardly believe that, for a butterfly moment, their lips had touched. 'You may be relieved to know that I did not believe a word that Nurse Bond told me. She is an excellent nurse and will be a great asset to Beatties if she goes into green, but I think you must have annoyed her in some way. I have no wish to know the details of any petty squabbles going on in the Nurses' Home, and I advise you to be careful when dealing with senior staff. Remember that she had years of experience before you came here and must resent young know-alls.'

'Is that the picture she gave you?'

'More or less,' he said.

'Well, well,' she said, and smiled. Then she remembered Kate. 'What happens now? Is Nurse Minter in trouble?'

'We've agreed to let the whole matter drop until Nurse Marne can be located. If, as you say, she took some of the tablets, it might mean that she has taken them at other times and will continue to do so, and we must find her for her own sake.' His face was grave. 'I have seen a lot of junkies in my time, and most of them began their downward drift when they took soft drugs casually, or smoked their first joint.' He rose to his feet. 'Come on, I'll buy you a drink. It's the least I can do. That is . . .' he looked at her closely. 'Are you all right? Should you be drinking alcohol?'

'Why not?' They reached the place where the path

divided, one branch going on to the Falcon and the other back to the hospital.

'Well . . . you know best, I suppose,' he said.

'For God's sake, will you get it into your beastly thick head that I am *not* pregnant?' She was furious. Her eyes glowed with angry fire, her lips parted and her breasts lifted with emotion. He took her firmly into his arms and kissed her with a fierce intentness that held passion and an undercurrent of sad yearning. 'Oh . . . you . . .' she began.

He released her and his smile was half devil again. 'Well, if you aren't, I can't see how you escaped until now,' he said.

She turned and ran from him, taking no heed of his shout. She ran on, her eyes blurred with tears, back towards the hospital. So he thought as badly of her as he had done from the beginning. He thought she was a slut. 'Oh!' she cried, the pain in her ankle making her catch her breath as she stumbled over the vandalised piping of the old fountain. He caught her up, as he had done on the night of the disco and carried her, struggling, back to Beatties. He held her tight against his chest and she could hear the level beat of his heart. The pain was less now and she stopped struggling.

He grinned his Mephistophiles smile. 'We'll have to stop meeting like this,' he said. He put her down on the sitting room couch and bent to take off her shoe. 'It's nothing,' he said airily. 'If you will run away from men in the park, you must expect to twist your ankle. Come on . . . bed for you.'

She sat up and tried to stand. 'I've never been attacked in the park before tonight,' she said icily.

'When I really attack . . . you will know it,' he said, and she shivered. What had Kate said? That when Mr Nicholas Smythe fell in love, meteors would fall, lightning would flash and all the world would know. She thought of Nigel, with his forceful, almost cruel approach to her, trying to win her. Were all men brutes? She felt the gentle fingers probing at her ankle, soothing and not paining her. This man was not like Nigel. So he teased her, he had a poor opinion of her and despised her as an easy lay . . . would he have taken it for granted in the park that she would submit to his demands?

She followed him, hobbling still. He put out a hand to steady her. 'A hot bath followed by a cold compress on that bruise and you'll be fine,' he said.

He left her at the bottom of the stairs and she went up, slowly. Suddenly, he couldn't bear to touch me, she thought unhappily. Even professionally, he had withheld his help.

The telephone rang in the hall and he answered it. 'Nurse Turner,' he said. 'For you. Hold on a minute, she's a bit slow,' he said to the caller. He came to her halfway up the stairs and picked her up as if she was a kitten. 'Boy friend on the phone . . . one of them,' he said, and deposited her roughly into the chair by the telephone. She picked up the receiver and glanced back, only to see Mr Nicholas Smythe striding away, the set of his shoulders showing again his dislike of her.

'Hello,' she said, and was silent as Nigel went on and on and on about the night of the dance.

She hardly heard a word. 'Dance . . . humiliated . . . load of morons as doctors . . . the sooner you come to your senses the better . . .' And she heard one sentence. 'I'm coming to see you tomorrow, and I shall make a bloody great scene if you don't come out with me.'

'I've nothing to say to you, Nigel. I'm off tomorrow evening at six and I'll meet you at seven. I can come out for only an hour as I have to study for my exam and I shall be coming only to say goodbye. So, if you think it's worth coming, I'll be at the entrance at seven. But make up your mind that I am not in love with you, never was and never will be!' She slammed the receiver down and found she was smiling. It was the first time she had managed to speak so forcefully to Nigel. I must be feeling more independent, she thought, or was it that I was upset by Mr Smythe?

With some difficulty, she got into the bath and tenderly soaped the offending ankle. He was right, of course, there was hardly anything to see. She did as he had suggested, however, and slapped cold toilet water on the ankle after the bath. It felt almost completely better when she tapped on Kate's door. 'Well? Has anyone said any more about the drugs?'

Kate grinned. 'Not to worry. I went to Sister Coates and told her what happened and your Mr Smythe was there. He asked a few questions and went off and I heard, from a very reliable source, that he and Nurse Bond had a blazing row. He threatened to make her apologise, even though it would be humiliating for a senior nurse, then he offered to straighten it all out. I expect you'll be seeing him.'

'I have,' said Jennifer shortly.

Kate looked at the bandaged ankle. 'Beat you up, did he?' She saw the blush and grinned. 'Only teasing. Did he chase you?'

'No, of course not,' snapped Jennifer, then the hint of a smile touched her lips. 'Not really . . . I tripped,' she said. 'Any news of Roberta?'

'Last seen hoofing it for the bus station. That was careless if she didn't want to be followed. She told me that she lived in Reigate and the buses leave for Surrey from there. Cheer up: she'll have to get in touch if only to say she isn't coming back.'

'Until she does, we aren't really off the hook.'

'Forget it. I intend to concentrate on passing my exam. I have no intention of being bullied out of this hospital by Nurse Bond or anyone unless I am so dimwitted that I really wouldn't fit in here. I wonder why Nurse Bond wanted to louse it up for you?' Kate was solemn. 'She was doing it for real, but I think she'll handle you with kid gloves in future after the rousting she had from Old Nick. Poor Bond. Did you know that she had been trying to persuade him to go home with her and go riding? He finally said he would go next week and she spread the good news around the hospital. Surprise . . . he didn't like it one little bit. He said so during the row and the date's off, so she gained nothing and lost . . . who knows what?'

'Riding? I thought . . .'

'I overheard that snippet, too. Did you think your dishy man was taken and they were planning the white satin and flowers? I confess I wondered.' She grinned. 'So there's hope for someone . . . maybe I'll take a crack at him.' She regarded Jennifer critically.

'I think you'd stand a better chance.'

'What rubbish . . . do you know, Kate, the horrible man thinks I'm pregnant!'

Kate hooted with laughter. 'And he's a doctor?'

'Don't be silly. He didn't examine me! He just put two and two together and made a hundred. He saw me faint, he heard I'd been sick in the morning and he obviously believes that I sleep with Nigel.'

'Who would do nothing to deny it,' said Kate drily. 'The man must be blind . . . you've got Virgin written all over you, Jen . . . nobody would take you for an easy lay, unless . . .'

'Unless what?'

'Nothing,' she said with infuriating calm. 'He's blind, that's all.'

'Sometimes you are infuriating, Kate Minter,' said Jennifer. 'Any ideas about finding Roberta? If she just opted out, the hospital would accept her resignation. It's a two-way arrangement. If they don't like us, out we go and if we don't like them, we leave and no hard feelings.'

'From what I hear, Mr Smythe wants to check up on her regardless of her rights.'

'So he does believe us,' said Jennifer. 'He thinks that Roberta might need help.' She frowned. 'I'd like to see her again. I like Roberta and I feel that, somewhere, she's had a bad time.'

'We could go down on our day off. I have her address,' said Kate, 'and I'm sure she went home.'

'We can study tomorrow evening and go to Reigate the day after,' said Jennifer. 'I think I'll mention it to Sister Jones. She may be able to suggest what we can say to her.' She made a gesture of annoyance. 'Oh, I forgot. Nigel rang and wants to see me tomorrow.'

'I thought you'd made it clear that you weren't interested?'

'He threatened to make a scene here if I don't see him. I told him that I wasn't in love with him, but he still wants to see me.'

'Well, bed for me,' yawned Kate. 'I ought to learn up the circulation system but I can't think straight tonight. See you in the morning.'

Jennifer tossed on the bed, trying to place her ankle in a comfortable position. It wasn't really painful but she was conscious of the discomfort even as she fell asleep. Sister said we must not only put a patient in bed, but we must make sure she is comfortable before leaving her. How very true . . . wish someone would tuck me up and kiss me goodnight, she thought, and dreamed of a man with a wicked smile . . . but he receded into a confusion of sound, of Nigel shouting over the telephone, Nurse Bond saying that Nurse Turner took drugs and a loud bell that clanged and forced itself into her consciousness. 'Oh, no,' she moaned. 'It can't be time to get up yet.'

Kate hammered on the door. 'How's the ankle?'

'Fine,' said Jennifer, turning it from side to side. 'No excuse for missing a lecture. I'll be down.'

The morning passed without incident. Kate asked Sister if they should visit Nurse Marne and, after consideration, she agreed that it would be a friendly and caring gesture. Kate told her that there was a bus at ten, 'You could have lunch at a very nice café I know,' said Sister.

'Not if I can help it.' whispered Kate. 'I'd rather have a ploughman's than boiled cabbage à la café.'

As the afternoon session finished and the apparatus was neatly put away ready for use again after the day off, Jennifer almost forgot that she had to meet Nigel. She had already told Charles that he was coming and that she wouldn't be available. His miserable look made her sad. 'Why not take some of the others? They're good fun,' she pleaded. 'You can't take me out all the time,' she added. 'I like you very much, Charles, but I haven't come to Beatties to have a love affair.' She felt very guilty but knew that if Charles was to be interested in another girl, she had to be definite.

'Does this mean you are going back to that creep?' said Charles.

'I was never with him, although he tried to make it seem so,' she said. 'But I must meet him once more to make him see how hopeless it is. I think he's more annoyed about not getting the teaching job because he isn't married than he is with me for refusing him.' She smiled. 'He's like his father in many ways. They are both go-getters who resent being thwarted. Nigel is bent on teaching as a means to long holidays and his father works him very hard in the estate business. It was a way out for him, but I'm not going to be blackmailed into marrying him to further his own ends.'

With those thoughts on her mind, Jennifer walked down to meet Nigel, who was leaning against his car parked outside the Nurses' Home in the area marked clearly 'No Parking'. Typical, thought Jennifer, and the sight hardened her resolve.

'Hello there, darling,' he said, and tried to kiss her in full view of the windows. She sidestepped and looked away. He scowled. 'Well, where shall we go?' She looked at the car. 'I thought it would be quicker if I parked here,' he said.

'Better move it, Nigel. It means what it says. Ambulances come this way and must have a clear run. I'm not coming until you've parked it where it should be, in the visitors car park.'

'But I'm taking you out.'

'No, I'll walk to the Falcon with you, have one drink and come back. I have work to do and I can't waste the whole evening. I am not coming in the car.' He strode away furiously, banged the car door and drove fast along the path to the car park. Jennifer smiled. If she had got into the car, she knew that nothing would have induced him to bring her back in an hour. Round one to me, she thought.

They walked in near silence to the Falcon. Jennifer insisted on having tomato juice and refused any of the exotic drinks he offered. She sat sipping from her glass and waited for him to speak. Even Nigel began to realise that he wasn't going to be able to smooth things over and convince her that what he had to offer was what she wanted. He said all the wrong things, quoting Mrs. Turner and the hopes she had of their marriage, stressing the fact that without her the job in the school was not available and trying to tempt her with the things she detested, the promise of a fur coat and a diamond bracelet to match the ring he had bought for her as an engagement present.

'You know so little about me, Nigel. Doesn't the

badge on my anorak, "Only rotters hunt otters", suggest to you that I would never wear real fur? And I'm really not the type for diamonds.'

He drained his glass and looked round for a barman. 'Come home when you have a weekend and we'll talk again,' he said.

She stood up. 'Stay if you want to, Nigel. I'm going. You haven't listened to me at all. I repeat that this is goodbye. I hate hurting you, but I don't think you are really affected. Your pride may be bruised a little, but you will find someone much more suitable to wear your furs and diamonds. I'm more comfortable in all the clothes you dislike; jeans and casual jackets, fishermans smocks and tee shirts and simple dresses, good colours but no frills. I'd never be able to live up to the things you like. Goodbye and good luck. I hope that you'll forget me very soon.' She turned and walked out of the bar, ignoring his call to her to come back.

She hurried back along the road, afraid to venture through the quiet park alone. The gates of Beatties had never seemed more welcome and the sound of the ambulance bell spoke not of drama, but of welcome. I hope we find Roberta, she thought. I couldn't bear to leave now. She saw a tall figure in a white coat hurry into casualty and she paused until he was out of sight. Mr Smythe had more important matters on his mind than the misdemeanours of very junior nurses.

CHAPTER EIGHT

It was an anti-climax after all the planning. Roberta had telephoned Matron to say she wanted an interview with her regarding her future and it was by sheer luck that Jennifer and Kate were stopped from going on a fruitless visit to Reigate. They resigned themselves to a day of study, which was perhaps more useful than taking time off to go on a trip. An air of depression hung over the sitting room where the new nurses pored over their books and tried to test each others knowledge on such weighty subjects as the circulation of the blood, the bones making up the human skeleton and the rules of hygiene.

It was a useful prelude to the exam, and when the rain began to fall at lunch time, Jennifer was glad that she wasn't paddling about in a mackintosh and umbrella, waiting for buses. Four of the set went to have lunch in the café by the Green and the rest stayed in the hospital. Jennifer wasn't very hungry and ate in the hospital cafeteria, settling for a salad and some coffee. 'Well!' she said, as she joined the queue and saw who was in front of her. 'Roberta!' She waved to Kate who had bagged a table and led Roberta over to join her.

'What happened to you?' said Kate. 'Are you all right? Are you coming back?'

'First, I want to thank you two for trying to cover up for me. I woke and found the bottle of barbiturates gone and dimly remembered that you had come in and taken them. I went into a panic. I thought you would report me and I'd be sacked, so I packed up and made some excuse to Sister that I was unwell and left. I didn't think any further than that.' She looked miserable.

'Have you seen Matron?'

Roberta nodded. 'She was terribly sweet and understanding. She really listened to me . . . that was a surprise. I thought that everyone would be down on me and not listen to any excuse.' She sighed. 'I knew I had done wrong, but I was prescribed that drug by my own G.P. and I'd forgotten to bring them. I've been so worried about the exam that I haven't slept well for a week. I was quite desperate and when I went to Ward 3 to learn about the lay-out of the cupboards, I saw the bottle and slipped it into my pocket. I was going to take a couple of tablets out and put the bottle back, but Sister had eyes in the back of her head and there was no opportunity. I was very tired, as I said, and when I was out with friends, I was given a double brandy. I came back and took the tablets, not knowing that they were twice as strong as the ones I have from home. I went out like a light, and you know the rest.'

'So you were entitled to take them . . . or at least a form of that drug?'

'When I was working at the psychiatric hospital, I had nightmares. I went through a bad patch and every time I saw the doctor, he gave me something to make me sleep. I wasn't hooked, but I did feel that I did my work better if I had a good night, so

in a way, I suppose I was on the way to dependence.'
She smiled. 'If I had been here, they would never
have prescribed that drug for a member of staff. Mr
Smythe was most emphatic that it was the fault of
the man who gave me them in the first place, and he
prescribed a simple tranquillizer to get me over the
next week.'

'You're staying? Oh, Roberta, that's good news.
From what Sister on Ward 3 said, I thought that
anyone who even looked at a drug here was for the
chop!' said Kate.

'I have Mr Smythe to thank for that, too,' said
Roberta. 'He told Matron that he had experience of
young people who made a mistake and suffered
unjustly for it for the rest of their lives. He was most
kind,' she said. 'He begged Matron to allow me to
take my exam and my month's trial. He asked her
to make it a trial of behaviour as well as ability,
saying that I didn't know the magnitude of my own
sin.'

'And what did Matron say?'

'She had my references there and the report from
the other hospital. They said that I had left because
I couldn't face nursing the mentally ill, but would
do well in a general hospital. They were all good
reports,' she added modestly. 'I'm so relieved that I
can stay and I know I shall be looked after here. If
the pressures are too great, I can ask for help or
leave the hospital. Matron said that if I didn't stay,
I could have a job in medical records and still serve
Beatties.' Her eyes were shining. 'But it was Mr
Smythe who convinced her that I must stay. I love
that man . . . I really love him.'

'Lucky Mr Smythe . . . love seems to follow him around,' said Kate with a laugh. Jennifer was silent. 'It's a pity that everyone in our set doesn't see his finer points,' Kate said. 'Jen thinks he's sarcastic and cruel.'

'You must be very ungrateful,' said Roberta. 'When Sister told Matron that you were the one who had the drug bottle, he was quite cross. He said it was quite ridiculous to imagine you doing anything to interfere with your career and that you weren't the type to play around with drugs.'

'He said that?' Jennifer stared in disbelief.

'He was very much on the side of us new nurses, and showed it,' said Roberta. 'I feel much more confident of passing the exam now. I'm going to my room to revise, so if anyone is staying in for supper, please give me a call.'

They filtered back to work and forgot the worries of the previous day as they struggled with medical terms, bedside procedures and simple trays and trolleys. After supper in the cafeteria, Charles came to the sitting room to help Jennifer revise anatomy. He soon had an eager group round him as he demonstrated the different types of joints and showed them illustrations of the tendons and muscles that were responsible for working them.

'Fascinating,' said Kate. 'I just bend my arm! I can't believe that all that goes on under my skin. If I want to pick up a book, I don't think twice, I just do it, and you say that messages from the brain tell the muscles to contract or relax as needed before we have finished thinking that we are going to do the action. Well, the more I learn, the more complex and rather frightening the human body becomes.' He explained patiently and grinned when someone thanked him, saying that he was learning more than they were.

'I think I know the outline, Charles. Sister didn't tell us half the things you've mentioned, and I don't think the examiner will expect much detail at this stage. It isn't as if we are taking our Prelim; this is just to see if we are capable of learning, Sister said.' One by one the nurses drifted away, to make coffee, to listen to the radio or to put out uniform for the next day. It was ten minutes to eleven and Kate asked Charles if he'd like some coffee.

'I ought to go,' he said. 'I am only a lowly student, unable to be trusted in the virgins' retreat after eleven.' He twirled an imaginary waxed moustache. 'When the clock strikes, watch out!'

'If you have instant coffee, it will take only a minute . . . that leaves four in which to drink it,' said Kate. She ran into the small kitchen and filled the electric kettle from the hot tap. Charles bent over the book that Jennifer held on her lap and pointed to a ligament in the illustration.

'What's that called? I know I've learned it, but I just can't think what it is,' said Jennifer.

'That one at the base of the leg, leading into the foot? That's the Achilles tendon. Remember your Greek mythology?'

'No, I was never very good at remembering who fought where in the Trojan Wars, who conquered who and who ran off with which goddess.' She laughed.

'Ignoramus,' he teased. 'Achilles was a famous warrior who was almost immortal. No weapon could wound him and it seemed that he was invincible, until someone whispered to the enemy that when Achilles was born, he was held in a stream that made him immortal, but he couldn't be completely immersed. He was held by one heel.'

'I've heard of an Achilles heel ... but I never realised it was based on that myth. A vulnerable point, a failing in some one. Well, well, one learns something of no use every day!' He made a half-hearted lunge at her. 'But thank you, Charles, I've learned a lot tonight.'

'And you know my Achilles heel?' His eyes lost some of the humour.

'No, I don't. I know you like to think you are getting fond of me, but it wouldn't do, my dear. I mean it, and I'm very fond of you.' She had to be frank, she knew what it was like to love someone who would never love her and if she could spare Charles from a similar fate, she would in some degree ease her own heartache.

'I thought that all students were forbidden in this sanctum after hours.' The devil's eyebrows were raised as Mr Smythe studied his watch. He smiled. 'What's your excuse, Mr Bird?'

'It's just eleven ... I've been giving the nurses the benefit of my superior knowledge ... Sir,' said Charles. 'I was thirsty and Nurse Minter insisted on reviving me with coffee.' He grinned and Jennifer saw that the two men shared a certain rapport.

'You may stay if I'm offered coffee, too,' said Mr Smythe. He glanced down at the book.

'I was learning about the Achilles tendon, Mr Smythe,' said Jennifer demurely.

'I see ... and did you discover your own?' The dark eyes searched hers, probing her inmost thoughts. She hid her eyes behind curling lashes and smiled faintly.

If he only knew what or who was her vulnerable area, he would run a mile, she thought. 'I know where my Achilles tendon is,' she said, deliberately misunderstanding his meaning.

'And how is it? How is the sprain?' asked the registrar. Charles looked from one to the other and Kate sensed the tension as she put the coffee tray on the table. 'Another cup, Nurse? Can you spare some for me?' said Nicholas Smythe, smiling.

'When did you sprain your ankle, Jen? I didn't know,' said Charles in an aggrieved voice, feeling left out of the conversation.

'Nurse Turner ran through the park, as if all the devils in hell were after her, I think.'

'I tripped,' said Jennifer, blushing furiously. 'I was ...'

'Frightened? Angry? Unable to cope with a very ordinary situation?' The voice mocked her. He's making fun of me again, she thought. Why pick on me? Why not goad some other nurse who wouldn't mind so much? 'How is it? Shall I examine it?'

'No,' she said. 'No ... thank you, it's better. I took a hot bath as prescribed and cooled it off with toilet water.' She made a determined effort and looked at him. 'I saw Nurse Marne,' she said. 'She's very grateful to you for speaking on her behalf.' She looked down again. 'I have to thank you, too, I believe.'

'You don't *have* to do anything,' he said coolly. 'I

lid and said what was needed, and tried to put the record straight. It does mean that you and your friends will have a certain responsibility towards Nurse Marne. I believe that we might have done a lot of harm if we had turned her out. She is slightly neurotic, but not unbalanced and, if you all help her and we make sure she has help if she's under strain, I think she will serve Beatties well.'

Jennifer saw the concern in the man's eyes. He cares about people, why not for me? He goes to endless trouble over patients and now Nurse Marne, but he looks at me as if I was a bad joke. 'I think I'll finish my revision in bed,' she said, and pushed away the cup. 'I'll wash up first, Kate, if everyone has finished.'

'And we must make a round . . . you are still on our firm, I take it?' said Nicholas Smythe to Charles. Charles reluctantly rose from his chair, watching Jennifer gather the used cups on to a tray. Mr Smythe waved a languid hand. 'Goodnight, thank you for the coffee, and remember that everyone has an Achilles heel.' He gave a sardonic smile and slapped Charles on the shoulder. 'Come on, I can't leave you here to help with the washing up . . . it wouldn't be proper.'

'He made sure that Charles didn't have you to himself,' said Kate. 'Not even the chance of a good-night peck!'

'What rubbish,' said Jennifer. 'Charles is a dresser on surgical and said himself that he's lucky that Mr Smythe takes him on the night rounds.'

'It keeps him occupied,' said Kate with a wicked smile. 'But it's quite out of keeping with my impres-

sion of Old Nick. I wouldn't have thought he'd b
the one to protect a young nurse from a fate wors
than death!'

'It's nothing to do with me,' protested Jennifer
'He can't bear to see anyone have a good time. If h
isn't the most important person on the horizon, h
sulks.' She didn't mean it and couldn't think wh
she said it.

'And was he sulking when he chased you throug
the park?'

'How did you know? I mean, he didn't ... I'r
going to bed,' said Jennifer, and escaped from th
sound of Kate's mocking laughter. It's bad enoug
worrying about the exam without being teased abou
a man who makes fun of me, she thought resentfully

The examination day arrived and the lecture roor
was neat and tidy, the desks bare except for th
sheets of clean paper ready to take the answer
required by the examiner, who turned out to b
nobody very frightening, only the sister tutor wh
took the first year student nurses in Block. Th
second hand of the clock touched the twelve and
rustle of papers marked the beginning of the tes
Jimmy, the skeleton, hung grinning in the corner a
Sister had forgotten to cover him while the test wa
in progress, and many glances went to him as th
anatomy questions emerged, so much so that Jennife
was convinced that Sister Jones, who was invigilat
ing, had left him there on purpose.

The hurried scratch of ball point pens and
flurried sorting of papers into sequence, togethe
with sighs of despair and grunts that could hav

meant anything, were the only sounds all the morning. The papers were gathered and checked, the bell sounded for lunch and a babel of voices rang through the building. Sister Jones smiled and left them to it. 'No post mortems,' she called. 'Be back here for your practical at two o'clock sharp.' She gathered her books and went to lunch, knowing that everyone would talk incessantly about the questions, the possible answers and the fact that it was a terrible exam. It happened every time, nobody admitting the possibility that she might have passed.

'Not too bad,' said Jennifer cautiously. 'When do we have the result?'

'We go away for a long weekend, come back on Monday morning and they tell us if we go on to a ward.' Kate sighed. 'A lovely long weekend, Friday, Saturday and Sunday. Do you realise, I haven't been back to the flat I shared with two girls when I was working in advertising? They said I could come whenever I liked and some of my gear is with them, so it's the bright lights for me, a blind date that Maggie fixed with her brother in the navy, and for two days I intend to forget that grinning creature in the corner who has ruled my life for so long. I know I got it wrong about the pelvis.' She looked at Jennifer with concern. 'Are you going home? Will Nigel be there?'

'I hope not. I think I told him plainly enough that I wasn't interested in any of his plans for me but, of course, I know if I ring my mother and say I'm coming home, she'll be on the phone to him in five minutes.'

'You haven't told them?'

Jennifer looked unhappy. 'No, I left it until th
last minute. I even considered staying here.'

'You can't stay here! You need to get away for
break. You've worked as hard as any of us and w
all need some light relief. What would you do
Mooch around and dread Monday? It isn't goo
enough, Jen. I know! You can come with me. I kno
there's a spare space. Have you a sleeping bag?
can lend you one and you needn't feel in the way a
we have lots of friends to stay from time to time.'

'It's lovely of you to suggest it, Kate, but
wouldn't work. You said you had a blind date and
would either have to stay at the flat, go to a cinem
alone, which I hate doing, or play gooseberry, whic
I flatly refuse to do.'

Kate smiled. 'You'd be doing me a favour. I ran
Maggie and she was in a tizz. Her brother is bringin
a friend and so she has an odd man. Do come, Jer
it will be fun. Maggie is very amusing and I've me
her boy friend. They're all right, I promise, an
you'll enjoy an evening with them. We can eat ou
and go window shopping tomorrow, sleep late o
Saturday and then meet them in the evening an
come back here on Sunday afternoon.'

'It sounds great,' said Jennifer doubtfully.

'It would be doing Maggie a favour,' said Kat
'Come on, see how the other half lives . . . the ma
world of advertising. I might get you into a com
mercial after all!'

Jennifer laughed. 'All right. I'd like to. I wa
dreading going home so soon after the row wit
Nigel. I know my family will be furious if I don'
marry him, and I'm not in the mood for a sermon.

It made all the difference. The idea of time off grew more appealing as she put away her books, and even the thought of bedside tests involving the hated Arabella didn't depress her. The afternoon fled and Sister smiled as Kate expertly stripped the bed and made it up, leaving the stiff dummy as comfortable as it was possible for her to look. Kate saw the smile and blushed, recalling vividly her first tangle, literally, with Arabella. The last bed was made, the last bandage folded and the exhausted school sighed with relief that this stage of their life at Beatties was over.

Sister Jones smiled. 'Go away and enjoy your weekend. I think you've earned it.' She turned in the doorway. 'And don't worry,' she said.

'Does that mean we've all passed? She can't know about the papers yet,' said Kate, 'but I'm sure she must think we've done quite well. I can't think when I've felt so pleased with myself! I know I'm going to stay at Beatties and I could easily miss out this weekend and begin on the wards.'

'Make the most of this holiday,' said Roberta. 'You'll need it. I know how tired a full day on a ward can be. I'm going home to put my feet up and I'm also going to rub them with surgical spirit to harden them!'

'Sounds as if you're going into pickle,' said Kate. 'Wouldn't eau-de-cologne do instead of back rub?' She laughed. 'Imagine going out on a date smelling like a medical ward!'

Jennifer packed a few things in a zipper bag, including a smart dress and high heeled sandals of a dark green that matched the colour of the trim on the pale yellow dress. She brushed her hair until it shone and slipped into a simple linen suit of coffee and cream with a pretty shirt to tone. Kate eyed her with approval. 'That suit can go anywhere,' she said. 'I think I'll show my legs too. Give the world a thrill.'

They chatted on the top of the bus and, as they went down the windy escalator to the underground, clutched at errant skirts while holding their luggage. Jennifer was lighthearted and as they went further away from the hospital, she began to think that the ache in her heart might disappear if she was in a place where Nicholas Smythe would not appear. It's only a physical attraction, she told herself, but failed to find any relief in the knowledge. It will fade as I get involved in my work and see other doctors as good-looking as he is, going about their daily duties. She concentrated on the day. This is good, she told herself. Whatever happens on Monday, this is good. She looked at Kate who was describing some of the more bizarre things they did in the training school to her incredulous friend. Kate was laughing, completely carefree, completely fancy free ... lucky Kate.

'And you wouldn't believe how obedient I am, would she, Jen? I absolutely grovel to anyone in authority ... yes, Kate Minter, who gives as good as she gets in the big bad world, says "yes Sister, no Sister", as meekly as a child in kindergarten.'

They drank strong coffee from huge mugs, admired some new posters that hung at random on the walls of the flat and laughed more than Jennifer could remember doing for months. 'When does your brother come on leave?' she asked Maggie when there was a lull, and was told that the three men were staying at a club and would meet them at the flat the following evening.

'So you see, Jen, it's good to have your company. We don't see them until then and I can show you some of my old stamping ground tomorrow. We'll get some Chinese take-away and cider and just talk tonight, if that suits you?' It was all so relaxed, so friendly and the hospital seemed light years away ... Nigel didn't exist and Charles was a warm memory. 'Jen? Where were you? Miles away. Maggie said she'd get the food. Do you want prawn or pork?'

They talked late into the night, and Jennifer smiled to herself as she thought of the guilt she felt in the Nurses' Home if she came in late and made a noise. It was a fact that certain rights had to be given up if one lived in a community. A very tired nurse or doctor had every cause for complaint if precious sleep was lost by people showing no consideration for others. The Home would be quiet now ... everyone asleep, except for doctors on call. She wondered if Nicholas Smythe was in bed, or was he still doing a late round? No operations tomorrow except for emergencies, so he had no pre-operative patients to see, to reassure and to comfort. He would do that very well, she thought. She imagined the dark eyes softening in compassion. She knew it was possible, but only for his patients. Had he ever looked at a woman with such gentleness ... with love?

'Wake up, I asked if you wanted more coffee,' said Kate. 'I'm going to sleep. There's a sun bed in my room which is quite comfortable, so slide in when you're ready.' She yawned. 'You've been in a dream for the past half hour, so you might as well dream for real.' She smiled. 'I'd like to know what goes on in that little head, but I'm sure you'll never tell me.'

It was a good unwinding. Sleep and conversation, food when they felt hungry and no work to do. Jennifer wondered how Kate could leave such a relaxed and unconventional life for one that needed such self discipline and a rigid timetable. She dressed with care for the evening date and found that she enjoyed the company of the young Naval Officers. 'I'm very hazy about rank in the Navy,' she said to Kate. 'I know about the Air Force as a cousin flies, and the Army is easy.'

'Not to worry,' said Kate. 'I never know the difference. They'll be in civilian clothes anyway. They like to get out of uniform whenever they are on leave, just as we like to dress in our own clothes. I sometimes think that if I wore those awful caps all the time, I'd have a cardboard personality to match!'

'At least tell me what they do? Are they basically engineers, sailors-on-the-bridge, or what?'

'Maggie's friend is an engineer, and so is my date, but the other is someone that even Maggie hasn't met. I have no idea what he does. Perhaps he's a leading stoker with tattoos over every square inch of skin. What a lucky girl you are, Jen!' teased Kate.

'I shall plead a headache and find a taxi,' said Jennifer firmly. 'One of the men in Ward 1 is covered with tattoos and a nurse who had to give him a blanket bath said he insisted on telling her where he got each one. Most embarrassing, she said, but she refused to go into detail.' It was good to go out in a group with people with whom she wasn't emotionally involved. The men were good company, easy to talk to and good-looking enough to make their presence a pleasure, and it was nearly three o'clock in the morning before they found a taxi to take them back to Maggie's flat.

'You haven't told me what you do in the Navy,' said Jennifer. The men groaned and refused to talk about work, making it sound as if they were ill treated, keel-hauled and generally overworked and underpaid.

'David is a doctor . . . that's all I know apart from the fact that the others are engineers,' said Maggie.

'I knew some of your men before I went into the Navy,' he said. 'Do you know Dr Spencer, on skins?'

'We certainly know Ward 3,' said Kate, with a meaningful glance at Jennifer.

'Let me see . . . who's working there on surgical? I nearly tried for the registrar job but decided I wanted to see the world first. I know . . . Nick . . . do you know Nick Smythe?'

'Yes . . . he's at Beatties,' said Jennifer, hoping that her suddenly fast-beating heart wouldn't give away the fact that under all the light conversation, the good company, his face was in her thoughts all the evening, his dark eyes reflected back through the dusk and his voice came to her out of the laughter.

'He's one of the best . . . good surgeon, good man,' said David. 'Pity he had that bit of bad luck.'

'Bad luck?'

'Didn't you know? It was common knowledge, but got a bit distorted on the hospital grapevine since it didn't actually happen at Beatties.'

'We know he was involved with a girl who died,' said Kate. 'We rather gathered that he was in love with someone who became pregnant by another man and died in a car crash.'

'He was very upset. He had been trying to get her off amphetamines . . . you know, the drug that keeps you going with a kind of false euphoria, and then lets you down with a bump, making it seem you need even more. Harmless in small quantities, but habit forming. He spent a lot of time with her, but she wouldn't listen. I think she was worried that she was pregnant and used the drug to give her spirits a boost. I think he felt guilty about her, although we tried to convince him that she was a free agent and that it was the responsibility of her lover and nothing to do with Nick.'

'If he loved her, he would be completely involved,' said Jennifer, more to herself than to the others. Unhappy, miserable . . . *lucky* girl, to have his love and concern, even if she died.

'I had quite a shock when I saw you, Jen,' said David. 'I hadn't thought of Nick or Pamela for months but, seeing you, it flooded back.'

'Seeing me? But you had no idea at first that I nursed at Beatties or had met Mr Smythe.'

'Don't you know? With that lovely hair and those golden flecked eyes . . . you're the spitting image of her.'

CHAPTER NINE

'I saw you before, didn't I? Only you had another colour dress. You passed your exam, I suppose, Nurse.'

Jennifer looked closely at the tall thin man who spoke to her. He was standing in the doorway to the sluice room and so she couldn't tell to which bed he belonged. 'Come on, Mr Gunter, stop showing off and get back into bed. You haven't been given permission to walk to the loo on your own yet. It's one thing to dangle your legs out of bed and be wheeled to the lavatory in a chair, but it's quite another thing to take risks, especially as you still have a tube in your wound,' said a nurse.

'Mr Gunter?' Jennifer could hardly believe her own eyes. He had been deeply jaundiced when last she saw him before he went to the operating theatre for an investigatory operation to see what was causing his condition. It seemed miraculous that he could have lost most of the yellow colour in his skin and even his eyes looked almost clear. The whites looked slightly muddy, but they had a sparkle that was lacking before his operation. 'You look so much better, I hardly recognised you,' she said.

'Would you fetch the wheelchair, Nurse Turner?' The staff nurse smiled and Jennifer was relieved to know that Nurse Pane had replaced Nurse Bond as the senior staff nurse on Ward 2, men's surgical. As soon as the exam results were known, a vague fear marred Jennifer's elation at having passed well. The idea of working on the same ward as Nurse Bond was daunting and she looked forward to her first day as a real nurse with some trepidation. The others were jubilant. Now, safely through the exam, they said that they had known all along that they had passed, the exam was easy, no true test of their capabilities and if the work was as easy, life would be a snip!

Only Roberta seemed to have the true picture. She was quietly confident and eager to start, but warned the others that it wouldn't be a picnic by any means. 'I do know what long hours and hard work can do, but to see people getting better because of what we do, fills me with pride, and I can't wait to begin,' she said.

As Jennifer walked on to the ward to report for duty, she was greeted by the nurse whose place she was taking, the girl who had served her month's trial and was leaving for Ward 10 after spending a day teaching her basic routine to the nurse fresh from the preliminary training school. It was strange to think that this girl had been on the ward for only a month, had passed her trial and now could be considered a full-time member of the staff of the Princess Beatrice Hospital. I'll never be as good as her, thought Jennifer, watching the easy manner and quiet skill that the girl brought to her work.

'Nurse Bond was the staff nurse here, and I believe she saw you when you came for the day,' said Nurse Pane.

'Yes, she taught us a lot,' said Jennifer truthfully.

'Is she still working on Ward 2, Nurse?'

'No, a vacancy came on women's medical and she went this weekend. All a bit sudden, but you know what it's like . . . or perhaps you don't.' She smiled. 'Her loss, my gain. I prefer to nurse men and I like a surgical ward, so I'm more than happy. Bond likes medical nursing and hopes to be a medical ward sister, so it follows that the powers that be will let her have as much experience as possible.' There was nothing in her manner to show that she had heard anything about Roberta, the drug bottle or any of the events before the weekend.

'I'm glad I'm working here,' said Jennifer.

'Just follow Nurse around today and go off duty this evening. You will double up today which gives you time to sort yourself out. I'll give you a full report after lunch and Sister will have a few words to say, no doubt, when she comes on at two.'

In spite of the fact that she had to make no decisions and that they were sharing the work, the day seemed complicated and long. The routine trips to sluice and ward were endless, the sight and smell of bedpans and urinals at first repelled her. At least Arabella didn't smell, thought Jennifer. But gradually, she didn't notice the smell of the sluice or of the disinfectant, and the sight of ill patients ceased to alarm her. She eased into the work and, at the end of the day, it was almost a shock to think that she had been hard at it for hours. The time had flown.

After lunch, Nurse Pane called the nurses into the office. 'The ward looks clear and I have time to go through the cases before Sister comes on duty and visitors arrive. It's about visitors I wish to speak first.

As you know, we allow fairly flexible visiting hours, but if a doctor wants to examine a patient or a treatment has to be given at a specific time, the visitor must be politely requested to wait in the day room until all is clear again.' She looked round the circle of faces. 'New nurses are particularly vulnerable, aren't they?' she smiled, as the nurse who was with Jennifer blushed.

'Yes, I'll never live it down,' she said ruefully. 'I don't mind you telling Nurse Turner, Nurse.'

'We have one patient who has been in hospital for months, in various wards, being investigated. He ended up here and we prepared him for operation. Nurse didn't know that he had been pre-medicated and so could have no visitors. He has a mother and sister who are very determined women! They had visited him in every ward, made a fuss about anything that didn't please them and generally poked their noses in where they weren't wanted. They told Nurse that they had special permission to visit behind the closed cubicle curtains and she let them stay. They gave him chocolate to eat and several biscuits because he said he had been refused breakfast.' She looked at Jennifer. 'Why was he refused breakfast?'

'Because he was due in the theatre and might be sick under anaesthetic?'

'That's right. Now, Nurse wasn't to know that the relatives would be so foolish but, in hospital, it is safer to take it for granted that everyone is a fool . . . and never accept that a patient knows what is best for him, without first checking with Sister, the doctor in charge, or me. Visitors are treated with courtesy and caution. Some people talk in an intelligent way but have the weirdest ideas of what goes on here. Fortunately, we found the traces of biscuit and he told us what had happened. He was very cross when the operation was cancelled until the next day, and his relatives were annoyed about it too, until Mr Smythe told them in no uncertain terms what might have happened in the theatre because of their lack of thought.'

Jennifer started at the mention of the name she hadn't heard since coming to the ward. She could imagine those devil's eyebrows raised in ironic disapproval. 'Rather them than me,' she said with feeling.

'Ah, yes, you've met our Mr Smythe, haven't you, Nurse Turner? I heard that he frightened the life out of you, but you know better than to unsterilise a pack now, I hope.' She regarded Jennifer with interest. 'I hope you don't scare easily. There are far more fierce men than Our Nick, and he's really a poppet.'

'Has he left the firm, Nurse?' asked Jennifer, half dreading the reply.

'No, he has a few days leave due and said he wanted to go home. Hinted that he had things on his mind.'

Sister Bendall came in and the staff nurse stood up. 'Carry on if you like, Nurse. I'll sit in and listen while you give a report. The ward is quiet, I've just whisked round and peeped into the side ward. Tell me about the new patients and then you can go. I'll fill in about the rest from the book.'

Jennifer sat enthralled. Nothing convinced her more thoroughly that she was a part of the hospital than this moment when it was taken for granted that she was responsible enough to hear very private and personal details of patients and was trusted to keep these facts to herself, to take a part in the treatment and, hopefully, the recovery of the people in the ward. She smoothed the already shining hair that sat neatly under the tiny, ridiculous cap and sat very tall. Her head buzzed with medical terms, she only half heard some of the prescribed treatments and wondered anew how anyone could quote so many facts about so many different conditions with such confidence and knowledge.

'Don't look so worried, Nurse. You don't have to run the ward entirely on your own, you know.' Sister laughed. 'Every nurse on her first day panics a bit, thinking that too much will be expected of her too soon. Believe me, we would much rather you showed very little initiative at first, to avoid mistakes. It doesn't matter how many times you feel unsure of what is expected of you, so long as you ask someone before doing what you half believe to be what is wanted. *Ask*, nurse, never try anything that you haven't been told to do. If any big bully like our Mr Smythe, demands your help, keep cool, tell him you must ask me, or Nurse Pane if you are in any doubt.' She laughed. 'He's a bit naughty sometimes. He teases the new nurses, but I think you've seen that for yourself. He is a first class doctor and surgeon and you'll love him.'

Jennifer smiled bleakly. If you knew how much, she thought, but not as the human, gentle doctor you all seem to know. Why must I be the one to feel the rough edge of his tongue, to see those devil's eyebrows meet in the middle as he frowns on me? To hear his chuckle of derision when I do something undignified?

She was conscious of an ache in the ankle she had turned. It had seemed quite better, but she supposed it was still weak. I'm tired, bone tired, she reflected, and when it was time to go off duty, she found the others of her set, draped over the chairs in the sitting room, looking as if they had worked non-stop for at least twelve consecutive hours. In spite of her own weariness, Jennifer laughed. 'What a lot of old crocks,' she said. 'I'm for a bath and some food.'

'My feet are killing me,' said Kate. 'I could do a commercial for those bath salts that cure sore feet. You know, the one where sharp stabs of pain come out of the joints, like arrows. I never thought it possible, but I can feel every tiny arrow.'

'You should have taken my advice,' said Roberta. 'If you'd rubbed your feet well every evening for a week with surgical spirit, they would be fine, like mine,' she said complacently.

'You can go off people,' answered Kate darkly. 'I'm going to bath and put on the sloppiest shoes I possess. I shall spend the evening in here with my feet on the table.'

They gathered again later, drank cup after cup of coffee and talked endless shop until, at a very early hour, they went to bed, to sleep deeply and be shocked into life by the morning bell.

'I now know what Sister Jones was on about when she told me I'd soon think my bed was the softest couch I've ever sampled,' said Kate at breakfast, stretching lazily. 'I just died last night.' She reached for the butter. 'One thing no longer worries me. I need all my calories for this job. I shall eat as much as I want, when I want it. It will be my one vice.'

The ward seemed quite familiar, as if she had been working there for more than just one day, but it was with a sinking heart that Jennifer realised she would have to do her jobs alone today. The other nurse had gone, the ward was busy and in spite of the encouraging words that Sister Bendall had spoken, it was very difficult to catch her or Nurse Pane to ask anything when the work was in full spate. The two blanket baths on her list were easy as the patients washed themselves all over and just needed backs rubbed and feet washed and dried. Mr Gunter was allowed to the bathroom in a wheelchair for the first time, care being taken to keep his dressing clean and dry, but he sat on a bath stool and managed a refreshing wash down that couldn't be done in bed. Jennifer was glad that he wasn't her patient as she had her doubts whether she could answer his rather vulgar repartee with coolness. He was the type of man who used obscene words as a matter of course, almost a punctuation to normal conversation and would have been shocked if anyone took any notice and objected.

Nurse Pane was very good and could banter with the most outspoken without loss of their respect. 'It comes with practice,' she said. 'I suppose it's a kind of defence. I was terribly shy when I was on my first male ward. We had several soldiers with orthopaedic operations. They were perfectly well except for the fact that they were strung up on Balkan beams and pulleys. They were young, bright and *very* cheeky.

My face didn't stop blushing for three weeks until I learned that they were taking bets as to who could make me react first! I soon learned that I had to make a shell, not a hard crust to repel people, but a small barrier of cheerful banter that has become part of the job and protects me from anything personal.'

'I'll never be like you, Nurse,' said Jennifer as a local Romeo whistled when she passed through the ward during visiting hours.

'Ignore it. Treat stroppy visitors to a dirty look and walk away. That's all right, but if he comes in as a patient, you'll have to cope.' She thought for a moment. 'Surprising, but true, they are quite different if they come in for treatment. I suppose they know they are in our clutches and they might as well behave. Scared, some of them, especially the tough guys who make a play for anything in skirts. It's really funny how someone who boasts can be terrified of the operating theatre while a little man like Mr Coombs over there will probably be quite calm and accept his fate whatever it is, with courage or dignity or both, whatever is needed.'

'Mr Coombs? What's wrong with him, Nurse?' Gradually, the faces were emerging from the nameless lumps that lay in the separate, white beds. It was becoming possible to go straight to several beds now without having to resort to the secret list in the pocket of her dress, giving the name and bed number of each patient in the ward. Jennifer was very grateful to the junior nurse who taught her to do this, although she warned her that Sister wouldn't be pleased if she discovered it a few days after joining the ward.

. 'Mr Coombs is suffering from a gastric ulcer. He's been in medical under Dr Pearce, the senior medical consultant, but he hasn't responded to diet or drugs, so there's nothing for it but surgery. He has a combination of symptoms which is rather puzzling and they aren't sure which operation will be done. If there is any doubt as to what will be revealed on opening the abdomen, they list it under Laparotomy, which means simply that they cut through the wall of the abdomen to see what's there.'

'But what if they find something that they aren't expecting, Nurse?'

Nurse Pane stopped arranging the trolley for theatre preparation and looked keenly at the new nurse. 'That's very perceptive at this stage of your career. Have you any idea about work in an operating theatre?'

'None at all, but I imagine the theatre staff lay up all the instruments wanted for a specific operation. They can't sterilize every single one, just in case they're needed, can they?'

'Sometimes it looks rather like that, but you're quite right. There is a basic set for each main operation, a set of subsidiary instruments for certain complications and so on. I worked in the theatre last year for three months but it isn't my scene. I prefer this type of work.' She smiled. 'See yourself wearing a gown and mask, do you?'

'I'd like it,' said Jennifer. 'But I'd be no good, I know. I've always wanted to be a theatre nurse, but I expect it takes a very definite kind of talent to be good.'

'If you think as you do now, there's no reason

154

why you shouldn't do it. Nurses from a surgical ward very often go to theatre early in their training as a follow on, so that they form a picture of the whole treatment ... operation and ward therapy.' She smiled. 'I'll bear it in mind, Nurse Turner. You may find yourself there sooner than you expect, as a spectator.'

Mr Coombs sat reading a newspaper, the picture of calm acceptance. He didn't turn a page in half an hour and Sister went to talk to him. At report time, she asked what they had noticed about him.

'He's very quiet,' said one nurse. 'He doesn't talk to the other patients much and he didn't want his lunch, Sister.'

'Nurse Turner? Any observations?'

'I thought . . .'

'Yes, Nurse, don't be afraid to say what you thought.'

'I thought he was too quiet. The other new patient, Mr . . . Barnes . . .'

'Good,' interrupted Sister, 'I'm glad you are giving names to each man. I can see that Sister Jones has done her work well.'

'He talks to the others and seems to want to find out what's in store for him. He's bound to worry, isn't he? I think that Mr Coombs is very frightened and is afraid to admit it, even to himself.'

'Right, Nurse. That is what I wanted to hear. I watched him with that newspaper. You can tell a lot from what a patient does when he thinks he's unobserved. He was still on the first page when I spoke to him after half an hour. A few words and it was evident that he had read nothing, not even the headlines.' Sister warmed to her pet theme. 'When you have time to spare in between duties, don't gossip about your boy friends in the sluice. You are here for the benefit of the patients. If you think one of them is lonely, talk to him. If Nurse Pane or I decide this is unnecessary and that you should be doing other work, have no doubt about it, you'll know soon enough! We never encourage idle gossip, but if we think you are needed at a bedside, gaining a patient's confidence, we will let you stay. It's an essential part of our work.

'But what do we say? We can't ask what's wrong, can we? He might resent any enquiry about his private affairs.'

'You don't probe, just be there, chatting, and with any luck you will find that he is only too relieved to see a friendly face and to have a stranger's ear into which he can confide something he couldn't tell to his nearest and dearest. That is our strength. We are professionals who can help him and who he may never see again in his lifetime. He can unburden his mind, make a fool of himself if he likes and we shall never tell anyone he knows, never point a finger of scorn at him.'

'But I'd be shy,' said another nurse.

'It's good to feel shy. I don't want you plunging in without any sensitivity. It's the really shy people, who suffer agonies when they have to meet strangers, who are often very good at this . . . take Nurse Pane, for instance.'

'But she's so self assured!'

'She's very shy but hides it. She's extremely good at gaining a patient's confidence and they like her.

I'm glad she came to this ward, at this time.' Was it imagination, or could Jennifer sense a double meaning in the words, as Sister glanced briefly in her direction?

'Do you want us all to talk to him, Sister?' said one rather matter-of-fact nurse in her second year.

'No, Nurse. That would be terrible if you all had a go at him. He'd imagine he was with the psychiatric unit! Just the nurses who normally do his treatment and make his bed.' She spoke briskly. 'I need to see each patient after being off duty for a day or two. I shall make beds with Nurse Jones on this side and Nurse Pane can take Nurse Turner down number 1's side.'

'I'll leave you to do the lockers on this side,' said Nurse Pane after bed tidying. 'Now you know who have drinks and who are on measurements. Are you quite clear about it?'

'Yes, Nurse.' Jennifer felt more confident after watching Nurse Pane and hearing her say the right words of comfort, banter or firmness as necessary. The patients appeared to like her and it seemed strange that men old enough to be her father or grandfather should accept what she told them with a meek, 'yes Nurse' and have faith in what she said.

'Nurse?' Jennifer jotted down the amount of fluid that one patient on measurement had drunk during the morning, and quickly went to Mr Coombs. 'Nurse, do you think you could post a letter when you go off duty? I'd like it to get there as soon as possible.'

'I'm not off duty yet, Mr Coombs, but I could pop down to the lodge when I go for my coffee break.

Claud, the porter, would post it or ask someone to pop it into the box, but I can't go outside the hospital in uniform.' She smiled. 'I'm sure it will go by the next post, Mr Coombs. Is there any other thing you want?' She glanced at the envelope. It was addressed to a firm of solicitors. The thought flashed through her mind. He thinks he's going to die! She looked round the ward for Nurse Pane but she was talking to the house surgeon. 'Mr Coombs,' she said hesitantly, 'I'd go now, but I have to wait until Nurse Pane sends me for my break.' She made it sound as if she was very nervous. He put out a hand and touched her arm. 'I'm very new, this is my first real day as a nurse,' she said.

'And you'll be very good,' he said, with more life in his voice than she had heard. 'Cheer up, my dear, I've seen new nurses before in the other wards, you know, and they all think they'll never make it.'

'We're both new, aren't we?' she said, 'but you've been in other wards. You know the sort of things that a new nurse does badly or wrong.'

He sat straighter in bed. 'That's right . . . I've seen them come and go and they all feel badly for a few days. I said to my son when he came to see me . . .'

'Your son? Is he coming?'

'No . . . that's what's worrying me, Nurse. I . . . I think there's something terrible happening in here.' He touched his abdomen. 'I told him I was better and he went off on a job to Austria. I couldn't bear it if I never saw him again. He's all I've got left. That letter . . . it's to my solicitor in case anything happens. I never made a will before and I must know

158

that everything is in order for my son. I didn't want him to worry about me.'

'And he'll worry all the more if you don't write to him and tell him about your operation,' said Jennifer firmly. 'How do you think he'll feel, if he has to find out when he comes home? He'll think you don't believe he cares about you. Or that's how I'd be if I was your son.' She smiled. 'Why not write to him, now? Tell him all about it, and about us. He'll be happier if you do. He'll be able to telephone and ask about you and in a day or so you can answer the phone yourself, from the telephone trolley.' I wish Sister was here, she thought. I'm probably telling him all the wrong things.

'I'll write, if you'll promise me something. Promise me that you will come to the theatre with me, just as far as the anaesthetic room if you can't come any further.'

Jennifer looked round wildly, and Sister saw her distress signal. 'Is something wrong, Nurse,' she said, in a whisper as she examined his chart.

'Tell Sister what I said, Nurse,' said Mr Coombs.

'Mr Coombs is worried because he hasn't told his son he is having an operation, Sister. I suggested that he might like to write now, and it can go to the post at the same time as this.' She held the envelope so that with a mere glance, Sister could see to whom it was addressed. 'Mr Coombs' son is in Austria,' said Jennifer. 'He could telephone if we gave the number.'

'That sounds sensible, Nurse.' Sister went to her desk and brought back a slip. 'Here is the name, address and telephone number for him. Here is the name of the staff nurse on night duty, the staff nurse on day duty and my name. He can contact any one of us, if that helps.' She smiled. 'Write it now and I'll send Nurse down to the lodge. Will twenty minutes give you time enough?'

'I'm sorry if I did anything wrong, Sister,' said Jennifer as Sister swept her away from the bed.

'Wrong? My dear girl, I couldn't get a word out of him. I knew he was worried, but I didn't know he expected to die! You did well, Nurse.' She saw that Jennifer was struggling for words. 'Yes, Nurse?'

'He said he'd write if I would go to the theatre with him . . . just as far as the door,' she added hastily. 'Of course, I didn't say I could.'

'Quite right, Nurse, but if he's taken a fancy to you and you give him confidence, I see no reason why you shouldn't go with him.'

Jennifer gulped. 'But Sister, he's having his operation in two days time, isn't he? I've never been near an operating theatre in my life, not even for adenoids!'

'You don't have to do the operation, Nurse,' said Sister, with a laugh. 'It will be very interesting. You can go with the porter and the trolley and stay in the anaesthetic room until the theatre staff take over. It shouldn't take long. There's no need for you to stay. Of course, we do allow a nurse to watch from the gallery or in the theatre if the video isn't in use, but not until she has been in this ward for about three weeks and, even then, we choose carefully. We want nurses to like theatre work, not to be put off by seeing it at an early stage and be frightened.'

'May I go there, one day, Sister?' There was no

doubt about her enthusiasm and Sister regarded her quizzically. 'I want to be a theatre nurse if I'm ever good enough,' explained Jennifer. 'I've always wanted it.'

'Let me see, the day after tomorrow . . .' said Sister. 'He goes to theatre as you go off duty. Do you mind giving up some of your own time?' Jennifer shook her head. 'Very well, you can go in with Mr Coombs and watch from the gallery. I'm sure that Mr Cardy will be pleased to have another member in his audience.' She smiled. 'He likes to lecture students, so don't be surprised if he pauses while the patient is well under and talks, waving his scalpel about in mid air.' She chuckled. 'He's almost as much of a character as Sir Horace Ritchie, our gynae man.'

'I wouldn't have to do anything, would I?' asked Jennifer.

'No, just keep out of the way. They are very busy in theatre and have no time to cope with people not involved with the work. Never attempt to do anything, just say you are a spectator, very firmly, if asked. More mistakes are made in any profession by well-meaning would-be helpers than by an army of trained people.' She glanced across at Mr Coombs who smiled and waved a sealed envelope. 'Hurry down to Claud and tell him the letters must go by the next post. He'll put them in the box down the road which will be quicker than waiting for the general collection from the wards.'

The letters were firmly in her hand as she hurried down the main stairs and out into the sunshine. It was strange to feel the sun on her back through the thin material of her dress. She didn't need a cloak as the air was warm and Jennifer felt a sense of accomplishment, of well being.

'You look cheerful.'

She started and saw Mr Nicholas Smythe standing by the lodge. Claud was just leaving his tiny box-like domain; she called him and gave him the letters.

'Cor! another one thinks he's for the chop,' said Claud brightly. 'Right, Nurse, I'll take them straight away.'

'An urgent letter to the boyfriend?' The sardonic gleam was back in the dark eyes.

'No, I hurried to get those to the post for Mr Coombs, a new patient on Ward 2, Mr Smythe,' she said demurely.

'And now?' The smile was lazy, appraising. 'Off to indulge in cloudy coffee and stale buns?'

He matched his step to hers. 'Something like that,' she said, not daring to look at him.

'Mr Coombs? Not the laparotomy for theatre this week?' She nodded. 'He's been with the medics for rather too long,' he said. 'I hope we can do something for him.' She looked up, startled to see the sombre expression. 'We'll do our best,' he said, and smiled as if it wasn't as bad as she imagined, or as he imagined, either.

'Mr Cardy is doing it, isn't he?'

'Yes, and I'll assist. Why are you so interested?'

'I have to take him to the theatre.'

'Well, keep from under our feet, there's a good little mouse.' He strode away, leaving her shaking with a mixture of fury and emotion, unable to retort.

If I go to the theatre, he'll know me this time. Just as I was getting used to the fact that he knows me as the girl with scraped back hair who wears grubby jeans to discos, and now realises I'm also the one with long fair hair, who resembles the girl he loved but despised, he'll find out that I'm also the girl who infuriated him the first time I arrived on a ward. I'll have to gown up and wear a mask . . . and he'll know that I have no brain, no competence, as well as being a frightened . . . mouse.

A reluctant smile was on her lips as she went back to tell Mr Coombs that his letters were safely in the box. His gratitude was pathetic and her eyes pricked with sympathetic tears. He must have suffered agonies, wondering if he would worry his son by writing. Nice, ordinary man, she thought. I hope he does well. He patted her hand and gave her a chocolate bar. 'You won't eat that sort of food before the operation, will you?' she said anxiously.

'I promise to do everything they tell me, Nurse. Do you know, I feel much more . . . safe, if you know what I mean. I'm just looking forward to it being over.' He brought out a book and began to read, soon becoming completely absorbed in the story.

CHAPTER TEN

'You will remember, Nurse Turner, that when you return to the ward, I shall expect an account of what you saw in the theatre, what you heard and were told by Mr Cardy,' said Sister Coates. 'I shall also expect you to be very careful what you say to Mr Coombs when you see him after the operation. I must be the one to tell him what they found, especially if the news is not good.'

'You don't think he's very ill, do you, Sister?' Jennifer looked worried. 'He looks fairly well and doesn't complain much, wouldn't it be better to leave him and see if rest would cure him?'

'He's had weeks of that in medical but his symptoms remain. He has a very enlarged liver, which could mean any of a number of conditions, including secondary deposits of a malignant disease, cirrhosis due to over-indulgence in alcohol, or liver disease. He has discomfort rather than pain but has had a raised temperature.' Sister looked puzzled. 'He says he doesn't drink more than a half pint of beer or a glass of wine with a meal, and he had no sign of malignant disease in his gut when he had a barium meal X-ray. Sometimes, a small ulcer can cause pain and not be seen in the X-ray, but that wouldn't account for the enlarged liver.'

'Shall I see if the porter's come, Sister?'

'No, Nurse, the theatre staff will ring down to the porter as soon as they are ready and he will come up.' She looked at her watch. 'I expect he will be here soon, but sometimes a case takes longer than planned or the patient is sent back early for one reason or another. It isn't always easy to judge when to give the pre-medication injection of omnopon and scopolamine or whatever the individual anaesthetist orders, so we have an arrangement with the theatre sister. She rings down as each patient leaves, telling us when to give the next-but-one patient his injection. In that way, unless something very unexpected happens, we know within a quarter of an hour when to send the patient up to the anaesthetic room.'

'And Mr Coombs has had his drug?'

'Yes. It works very well if we all cooperate. I have been in hospitals where the drugs are given when they were ordered . . . and the poor patients nearly recovered from the pre-med. before getting as far as the theatre. It doesn't help the patient, the surgeon or the anaesthetist if the patient is very much awake and becoming anxious. You will see that Mr Coombs is very drowsy and a little high. He couldn't care less if it rained or snowed!'

The lift gates clanged and a trolley could be heard pushing between the double doors at the end of the ward. A porter, in a long white coat and white mask, unfolded the blanket and Sister and Nurse Turner stood ready to help lift the sleepy man on to the trolley. He opened his eyes and smiled when he saw Jennifer walking beside the trolley but was nearly asleep when they reached the operating theatre.

The small ante-room was softly lit and smelled of ether and antiseptic. A man in a green gown and mask and white theatre boots walked into the room.

He glanced at Jennifer and smiled and his eyes were warm and friendly. She knew that this was Dr Boris Pilatczech, the popular anaesthetist who had married a Beatties nurse. He suggested that she should ask the anaesthetic nurse for a gown and mask, 'That is, if you're watching,' he said.

The long white gown still held the creases of the packing and reached to the ground. Jennifer felt engulfed and fumbled badly as she tried to tie on the cap that came completely over her hair. The mask was easy, after the many times she had worn one while watching dressings on Ward 2 and she arranged it comfortably, recalling the first time she had worn one when it hurt the bridge of her nose. At least I shall be anonymous in this get up, she reckoned. She stood away from the trolley while gentle hands injected the drug that would send Mr Coombs quietly into deep unconsciousness before he knew he was near the theatre.

A laryngoscope was inserted into the mouth of the patient as a means of introducing a flexible tube into the larynx, making sure that the free passage of air and anaesthetics could be allowed at all times, during what might be a long operation. Jennifer was amazed at the speed of this procedure, the gentleness of the touch and the little affect it had on the patient, who was asleep and breathing deeply in seconds.

A kind of magic seemed to surround the main characters in the scene. There was calmness, efficiency, certainty of what they were doing, and a kind of love which made her want to cry as she watched them.

The doors opened. Suddenly, the big room lay

ahead with the bright lights blazing down on to the bare, gaunt table in the middle. The trolley swept in and all that was missing, Jennifer thought, was a roll of drums. In its way, it was a spectacular entrance, taken completely for granted by the staff.

A covered trolley was wheeled to the side of the operating table as soon as the patient was secured in position. A white-robed figure took away the empty patient's trolley and the doors sighed softly together again. Jennifer looked about her, startled. The gallery was empty, the light dim and two students stood, dressed as she was, in the theatre itself. A moment of panic as she realised that she was to watch, not from the gallery, safely away from patient, surgeon and assistant, but within shouting distance of anyone who thought she was doing something wrong!

The sound of water running down a shute ceased abruptly. The hiss of the sterilizers and the faint hum of the air conditioning were the only sounds and the theatre sister walked from the scrubbing-up bay with her hands held high in their soft rubber gloves. She glanced round the room, missing nothing. She looked hard at Jennifer and nodded as much as to say, 'All right, as long as you stay there, well away from the trolleys.' She uncovered the first instrument trolley and took sterile towels into her gloved hands, laying the green linen neatly across the foot of the patient. The whole of the exposed abdomen was painted bright orange and surrounded by a square of towels, clipped into position by small towel clips.

Two tall figures emerged from the scrubbing bay, the spectacles of Mr Cardy glistening above his mask.

The other eyes were not covered, but seemed to glow dark fire above the green mask, like a satyr peeping over a laurel bush, thought Jennifer, stifling a hysterical impulse to giggle. Her breathing was uneven, her heart pounded as he strode to his place on the other side of the table, putting out a hand to Sister who, as silently, passed him artery forceps and swabs. Mr Smythe looked round the theatre as he waited for Mr Cardy to make the first incision. He smiled at the staff nurse who was chalking up the total of swabs in circulation, said a word or two to the sister and then saw the slight figure standing apart, dressed in shapeless gown, her bright, gold-flecked eyes shining over the white mask of the spectator.

And she knew he recognised her as the girl who had unsterilised the pack and brought the ward sister's wrath down on him. She turned as if to go, her one thought to get away, to avoid having to endure any more of his sarcasm or displeasure. 'I see that you have students here today, Sir,' said Nicholas Smythe. 'Do you think they could come a little closer? The gallery is out of use due to an electrical fault, I believe.'

'Oh, who have we here today?' Mr Cardy turned to the two students. 'Ah yes . . . I know you. Glad to show you a very interesting case.' He spotted Jennifer. 'I don't know you . . . who are you . . . fish or flesh, male or female?' The students laughed dutifully. It was his standard joke. 'Well, speak up . . . we have no strangers, set my mind at rest. Do I want you in my theatre, eh?' He gave a fruity laugh as he saw the blush on the only exposed part of the girl's face. 'Ah . . . it blushes so it must be female.

Tell me, is there a figure worthy of those pretty eyes under that awful gown?'

'Everything in its place, Sir,' said Mr Smythe in a level voice. 'And do you think the patient might like to know his fate sooner, rather than later, Sir?' He's taking the heat off me, thought Jennifer. Mr Cardy must be the type to tease new nurses, but why should Mr Smythe try to deflect his attention? He is usually the first to be rude to me.

'You're right, of course, Nick. Nurse whoever-you-are, come closer and watch if you are really interested.' His tone was now kind and businesslike. He pulled the blade over the stretched skin and a fine line of blood followed it. Nicholas Smythe swabbed and the area widened rapidly. Jennifer watched, fascinated, as forceps were applied to each small bleeding point. The operation area was never allowed to become a gory mess as she had feared and the theatre sister seemed to know exactly what was needed, handing cat-gut for ties, the sterilised diathermy electrode to seal lesser bleeding points that might give trouble if left but which were too small for tying off. Warm towels wrung out in normal saline were packed round the skin edges before a large self-retaining retractor was gently inserted and opened, showing the inside of the abdominal cavity.

'Sucker,' said Mr Cardy. 'There's fluid here.'

The whine of the sucker machine settled to an organised gurgle and the inspection bottle showed red and then clear fluid as the flow slowed down. Feel this, Nick,' said the surgeon. He swabbed and cleared the area, stood aside and Nicholas Smythe put an exploratory hand inside the wound. He felt the liver and looked down as he gently pulled the lower level of muscle a little more to one side.

The theatre staff seemed to hold its breath. This was the moment of truth when they would know if Mr Coombs, the figure under the sheets who had lost his identity as soon as he lapsed into unconsciousness, was to be cured or to suffer more and perhaps die. Jennifer prayed desperately that the man would see his son again and lead a normal life once more. She gazed at the dark eyes over the green mask and saw the relief of discovery there. He looked across the table and smiled . . . smiled at her in the midst of all the tension. It was like a warm hand holding hers, telling her not to worry. This time, his concern included her.

'Abscess,' said Mr Smythe.

'Right . . . he did have an infection abroad a few years ago. God knows who tested him and what they gave him, but they obviously gave him an antibiotic and didn't drain the abscess, so he's carried around a sterile bag of pus all this time.' He pulled out the cooling packs. 'Let's have some fresh ones, the large sucker-end and be ready with the saline in case it spills into the abdominal cavity. Put a couple of clamps on each end . . . you hold that,' he said to the dresser by his side, 'and if you dare let them sag, I'll have your guts,' he added, in a friendly tone.

The sac containing the abscess was surrounded by a wall of towels, Sister had a line of swabs in the end tray, ready to exchange for the soiled ones as they came back to her, and the dirty nurse stood ready to take the soiled ones to check against the total on the slate, shaking each one out so that it couldn't possibly be mistaken for two, stuck together, and hanging them in line on the rack. 'Now, sucker on, Sister.'

The gurgle began again and thick green discharge came sluggishly down the tube into the bottle. As soon as the flow stopped, saline was injected little by little, and sucked back until the resultant flow was clear. The area was swabbed carefully, a drain sewn into position and the swabs were counted and double checked before Mr Cardy put out a hand for the right cat-gut, incorporated in an eyeless needle for sewing the first thin film of tissue. It was all so right ... so organised. Jennifer wondered what would have happened if the wrong things were handed to the surgeon, but the Sister seemed to know what Mr Cardy needed, even before he knew himself!

Stronger cat-gut on a round-bodied needle was handed for the first muscle layer and Mr Cardy turned away, peeled off his gloves and said calmly, 'Finish for me, Nick. I said I'd meet Sir Horace for a round, this afternoon. Purely business,' he chuckled, 'but we both need the exercise.' Mr Smythe moved over and took the nylon sutures and began to sew the skin, carefully making sure that the skin edges were turned out slightly to allow immediate healing with the least possible scar.

Mr Cardy came back into the theatre, without his gown. 'Nice job, Nick,' he said. 'He'll be more comfortable without that lot. Will you tell him? You know the drill. Drain into a closed bottle and nurse in high Fowler's position until the gubbins has gone.'

It was all so casual, as if he was saying, 'I'll just pop out while you put the kettle on,' when Jennifer wanted to shout for joy that the patient was going to be all right.

'There's coffee coming, if you've time, Sir,' said Sister. He nodded and went to change into his suit. Jennifer watched as they put Mr Coombs on the trolley and then she went into the nurses' room to take off the gown and mask and fix her own cap in place. She offered to go back to the ward with the porter and the theatre nurse to help lift at the ward end, and waited for the trolley to appear in the corridor. The doors swung open and Mr Smythe was bending over the patient, the green mask hanging from one ear, his gown gone and his chest bare to the waist.

He helped to guide the trolley out and saw who was waiting. 'I know you,' he said. 'Do you wave a magic wand. You disguise yourself pretty thoroughly.' He seemed put out, she thought. 'I get used to one Nurse Turner, only to find there are others.'

'And this one is the one you dislike most,' she said. The porter took the foot of the trolley and started off along the corridor. She ran to catch up, leaving him staring after her. He has a mole on his left shoulder, she thought. I wonder if the other girl with long hair saw it . . . touched it . . . kissed it?

She told Sister what had happened. 'I could tell by your shining eyes that he is going to be all right,' Sister said, 'but you must learn not to take anything too much to heart, Nurse, for good or evil. You are here to serve but not to give yourself. You must learn to do your best, with professional tenderness, which is far removed from being subjectively involved.

Do you understand?'

'But Sister, I couldn't be unmoved by the fact that Mr Coombs is going to be cured, could I? He's such a nice man.'

'You've a great deal to learn, Nurse. What would have happened if he had been told he was inoperable? If they had shaken their heads in the theatre and closed the wound without disturbing whatever they found there? Would you have been able to come back on duty tomorrow and face him?' Jennifer turned pale. 'Be pleased, of course . . . we all share that, but you must control your behaviour. Calmness at all times in the ward, Nurse, even if the news is very good. Supposing that the patient next to Mr Coombs went to the theatre on the same day and it was an 'open and close'. If you showed your delight about one patient, could you control your depression about the other, or would it show?'

'I see what you mean, Sister,' said Jennifer humbly. 'I don't know if I have that courage.'

'That's why all communication of results must come from experienced staff, staff nurses, sisters or doctors. Even junior house surgeons have to be warned about the personal side to medicine. It's something you can't learn from text books but it means more than much of the technical treatments you will have to give.' She smiled. 'You went in at the deep end a little too soon, I think, but I hope it hasn't put you off theatre work?'

'Oh, no, Sister.' Her eyes shone. 'More than ever, I want to do that.'

'Well, well,' said a sardonic voice. 'Ambition in one so young? My stitching met with your approval,

173

I hope?' The dark eyes were smiling. He's as delighted as I am, she thought. He cares about people. A familiar ache in her heart made her turn away. 'You didn't approve. I can tell. I thought I did rather well,' he said.

'You did . . . everyone was so good at their jobs.'

'And you felt inadequate? Well, that's a start.' She glanced up but he was smiling enigmatically. 'I began to think of you as "La belle Dame sans Merci".'

'Keats,' she said, in wonder.

'I didn't catch that . . . is he teasing you again, Nurse Turner? You mustn't take any notice of him.'

'I try not to, Sister. May I go now?'

'Of course, you are off duty, but remember what I said. No great detail when you see Mr Coombs until we make sure everything is going to be all right. Any operation is a risk and it isn't possible to rule out complications at this stage. Surgical shock, secondary haemorrhage, acute embolism . . .'

Jennifer made her escape. The fresh air was marvellous. She felt as if she couldn't get enough into her lungs. The others of her set were off duty and gone she knew not where. In a way, she was glad to be without their eternal shop talk and giggles. Today, she had seen something that made her aware of life and death which she had never before considered seriously. She went into the sitting room and flung her cap on a chair. A cup of tea would be good . . . she didn't have a real headache, but there was something, a sad tension. He thinks I'm a little know-all, to add to my sins, and yet . . . he quoted Keats. 'La Belle Dame' . . . it was a hazily remembered line from her schooldays.

She went to the glass-fronted cupboard and looked at the dull leather spines of books given to the hospital by benefactors who couldn't bring themselves to dispose of valuable books they never read. There were ancient medical books, nursing manuals well-thumbed, and a set of Dickens in dark brown leather bindings. She looked at the smaller books, piled haphazardly in one corner, and selected an old copy of *Palgrave's Golden Treasury*. She smiled as she riffled through the yellow pages and glimpsed many poems she had learned at school, ruined for her for ever by the too strictly analytical approach of the English master.

He had never done 'La Belle Dame,' and she found it and read it with a sense of discovery. It was fresh and unspoiled and she wondered why she didn't read more poetry.

She caught her breath. She must have been like this ... the other girl with long hair. She read to herself,

> I met a lady in the meads
> Full beautiful ... a faery's child,
> Her hair was long, her foot was light,
> And her eyes were wild.

And was it true as it had been with the Knight? When the maiden had him in thrall ... he awoke and found himself alone on the cold hill's side?

> And this is why I sojourn here
> Alone and palely loitering.
> Though the sedge is withered from the lake,
> And no birds sing.

175

He must have loved her very much, she thought with a sense of deep loss. What chance had any other woman of filling her place if he still thought of her like that?

The whistle of the kettle brought her mind back to the cup of tea she had promised herself. Perhaps Kate or one of the others was still in the Home. She walked slowly into the kitchen and nearly collided with the man coming out. 'Careful . . . is that all the thanks I get for making tea?'

'You didn't make it for me,' she said, wiping the milk spilt on her dress.

'Don't be so scratchy. I thought you'd need one, and I know I do. Sister has a noxious type of coffee in theatre. Mr Cardy thrives on it, but it's enough to give a rising young surgeon nightmares.'

'Oh, that accounts for the poem,' she said demurely. 'I suppose you dream of ". . . pale kings and princes too, pale warriors, death pale were they all . . ."'

'You haven't finished it,' he said quietly. 'They cried, La Belle Dame sans Merci has thee in thrall. You know it?' She saw him glance at the poetry book. 'I see you looked it up . . . how practical,' he said flatly.

'She must have been very lovely,' said Jennifer, not bearing to see the sudden anguish in his eyes.

'Very,' he said. 'Here you are, milk in the cup this time. He handed the cup of tea and pushed over a biscuit tin. 'Well, now you know all about hepato-megaly I hope,' he said, returning to his brusque manner.

'Do I?'

'You were there. It only means an enlarged liver, but it sounds impressive.' He laughed. 'You were like a cat on hot bricks when the boss began on you.'

'I wonder he finds time to tease nurses when he has something important to do,' she said warmly. 'Well, he had an important operation to do and he was . . . laughing. He also swanned off before it was over to play golf with someone.' She tried to sound indignant to justify her outburst.

'It might not have occurred to you that he was worried?' She shook her head, incredulously. 'It wouldn't strike you as strange that he had no idea what he would find? That the X-rays showed nothing because it wasn't a growth of tissue and the abscess was tucked up under a fold of liver and could have been anything in a picture? He had a man with a grossly enlarged liver, or so it seemed, and it might have been inoperable. We looked for a primary growth and found none and it puzzled us all.'

He smiled coldly. 'So Mr Cardy took time to let off a little tension by chatting up a nurse . . . do you begrudge him that light relief?'

'Of course not,' she said. 'But afterwards? Couldn't he have waited?'

'He was telling me in a way that I would understand and would not spread it around the theatre until the right time, that he has a patient who we think may be suffering from a gynaecological complaint, not a general surgical condition. He wants to talk about it to Sir Hector, who is our very brilliant senior consultant in that field. He retired officially a short while ago but still does private surgery and gives time to a V.D. clinic in Southwark for which he is *not* paid. This patient is a very well-known person who wants to keep out of the news and has every right to do so. She is a very pleasant, hard-working politician who deserves any privacy we can give her. There's nothing sinister in keeping it all quiet, just a very tired woman who should have come to us months ago.'

He's doing it again, she thought. This time, I suppose I asked for it but he does put me down at every opportunity. 'Thanks for the tea . . . and the lecture,' she said. 'I have to get changed.'

'You have a date?'

'Yes,' she lied. 'As a matter of fact I have.'

'Charles Bird is up to his eyes with notes,' he said helpfully. 'So it can't be him.'

'Does it matter who it is? There are other men who might want to take me out,' she said angrily.

'I don't doubt it,' he said with an irritating grin. 'Your fiancé, perhaps?'

'No . . . I mean yes . . . I'm meeting him in half an hour.'

'Then you'd better be ready.' he regarded her solemnly. 'Off you go, little mouse.' He picked up the tray. 'No . . . I'll see to this. I wouldn't have you miss your appointment.'

Jennifer ran to her room. If that insufferable, wonderful man was still downstairs in half an hour, she would have to go out, all dressed up as if hurrying to meet someone. She glanced at the clock. It was too early to eat out in the local café and she hated eating alone in public. The cinema . . . Oh, no! the local one was closed for repairs. The Falcon wasn't open and she would either have to go for a walk round the uninteresting streets or go out one door and dodge back in another. There wasn't even the sanctuary of the house up the road as it was closed to give the catering and cleaning staff a break before the next batch of student nurses arrived.

She flung her jeans back into the cupboard. She couldn't wear them. If he was still waiting, checking up on her, she must look as if she was going somewhere smart. She selected a dress made of pale turquoise silk, a present from an Uncle who lived in Malaya and had exquisite taste. It had been made up quite simply by the dressmaker at home and fitted beautifully. Her mother would have approved if she had worn it for Nigel's benefit, but he had never seen it.

Well, I can wear it in memory of a great escape from him, she thought. He'll never dare try to contact me again, surely. She smiled wickedly. I'll really dress up, she thought, and swan out of this place on a wave of expensive perfume. She added gold earrings and a gold and turquoise bangle and brushed her hair until it shone like a golden nimbus round her head. The ends curled up, gently loose after the confining duty style. High-heeled sandals showed off the sheer tights on the slender legs and she whisked a soft pale lipstick over her lips. She frowned into the mirror. What a waste . . . what a pity she had no marvellous man to take her out.

The hall was deserted and it was with a sense of anti-climax that she saw Nicholas Smythe was not here to be impressed by the care she took over dressing for her 'fiancé', or for any man who treated her as an adult, a woman, a desirable woman. She walked slowly to the door. Better go through with it. She could go on the bus and see if Maggie was in. It would give her some purpose.

The evening sun slanted down across the drive, catching the tree tops in a film of brightness. The park would be good, but it wasn't for her on her own. 'Alone and sadly loitering,' she said, sadly. It wasn't only the knight in the poem who did that.

A man who was bending over the open bonnet of his car straightened. She gasped. Nicholas Smythe wore a light cashmere sweater and well-tailored trousers. His eyes were dark over the pale blue and laughed at her surprise. He looked at her with approval. 'I like the dress,' he said. He looked at his watch. 'Dead on time, and very nice too.'

'What do you mean? I have to go, I'm in a hurry,' she said, half expecting Nurse Bond to emerge from the Nurses' Home. Why else would he be there, so obviously waiting for someone? From what she had seen of the other doctors, they didn't dress up if they were meeting each other for a drink, a meal or talk shop. She half smiled. He was rather beautiful, and he was so pleased with himself. I hope he's got over the other one ... I hope he'll be happy with the new lucky girl, she thought, with a pang of envy. 'Goodbye.' She turned away, but he called her.

'I forgot. There was a telephone call for you. Silly me,' he said, in a tone that left her in no doubt.

'You didn't forget,' she accused. 'Who was it?'

'Your fiancé. Said he couldn't make it.' He grinned and the devil showed in his eyes.

'I don't believe you . . . you couldn't have done. I haven't said . . .'

'You didn't have a date with him? My, we are both very forgetful today.' His voice was mocking but his eyes were merry. 'I shall have to try to console you for his absence.' He held open the car door, but she hung back. 'You're teasing me again,' she said. 'I never know when you are laughing at me, and when you merely dislike me!'

'So that's what you think. It's high time we compared notes and decided just what we think. I can't work with people who either don't trust me or dislike me as much as you seem to do,' he said. 'It's bad for business. And we can't have Ward 2 disrupted by such undercurrents, can we?' He beckoned and she was powerless to resist or to do what her fast-beating heart warned her would be wise.

'You're almost as much a bully as Nigel,' she said, with the remnants of her spirit. What on earth could he have to say to her that couldn't be said on Ward 2? If he wanted to tell her off for her manners, he didn't need to dress like that . . . to look like that, and be so close to her in the smart two-seater car.

'Ah, yes Nigel,' he said, and fell silent.

'Where are you taking me?'

'Well, first of all, I thought that we'd have a nice quiet, country walk near Dorking.' He saw her horrified expression. 'Then, on second thoughts, when I saw the quite enchanting but wholly useless sandals you are wearing and the fact that Dorking is a little close to home for you, decided that the canal would do.'

'The canal? Have you seen it lately? Dead cats and sewage.'

'Not this one, Don't get alarmed. It is in the direction of Surrey, but the stretch I mean has been cleaned up. Hardly one dead cat, and you can walk without tripping over a sack of coal.'

'But I was going up to Town. I was going to meet a friend of Kate's.'

'Oh yes?' he said politely.

'Just because I told you I was meeting Nigel when it wasn't true, doesn't mean that I had no plans for this evening. Maggie has some very pleasant, polite and attentive friends who I met with Kate and like very much.'

'Maggie? With Kate in advertising? Mass of red hair and too many freckles?'

'She has red hair,' said Jennifer, cautiously. 'Was that a guess or do you know her?'

'Of course I know her. I know every one of consequence.' He grinned, and she knew he was teasing again. 'I know Maggie's brother and his best friend, David.'

The light dawned. 'Of course . . . you do know them. David told me he had worked with you.' She thought fast. David had also told her about the other girl, Pamela. 'He did mention you,' she said.

'And nothing more? No more than "I know Nick Smythe . . . is he still alive"?'

She looked ahead at the gaunt old houses that had once been warehouses but were now restored and turned into expensive flats. The broad walk by the canal was newly laid and edged with flower beds, the whole area hinting at new life, new wealth and a feeling of brightness so foreign to the old wharves. 'It's a miracle,' she said.

He drove into the car park of an inn and stopped the engine. 'Miracles do happen,' he said. He went round and opened her door, handing her out with exaggerated ceremony. She smiled. If he wanted a light-hearted evening, a kind of truce, she would play up to him.

'Merci, Monsieur,' she said, inclining her head gracefully.

He ordered real ale and they chose food from the wide range of cold roasts and snacks available. It was warm enough to sit outside, sheltered from any breeze by a frosted glass partition and a light awning. The water glinted wickedly as if it knew all the secrets of the canal and many more. A barge disturbed the glassy surface, sending concentric ripples to the banks, ruffling the green plants that grew out of the old walls.

'You've been here before tonight?' It was something to fill the silence, but she regretted the words as soon as they were said. 'I mean, it can't have been like this for more than a few months ... how did you find it?'

'I came a few weeks ago with some friends. We found it quite by accident. We thought there must be a pub of sorts as I've yet to find a waterside place without one, and this is what we found. It's still not finished and I hope they don't sacrifice the atmosphere completely in the cause of cleanliness and progress, but it's a good place to bring a girl for an evening.'

He couldn't have brought her here ... it didn't exist when she was alive. The conviction that this was a new place for him, a new start, made her

uneasy. Had he brought Nurse Bond here? Was sh
in the party who discovered it? She wanted to be th
first girl he brought to the place, to stamp a little o
her personality on it before he brought the girl h
would love . . . a pale ghost, looking in through th
flawed glass of the screen. 'Can we walk here? Yo
seemed to think that even my sandals would stan
up to it.'

They went down to the water and he produce
some bread he had taken from the table. A pair o
swans, pure white necks arched and cautious, cor
descended to accept the bread, swimming in sma
circles, dipping their yellow and black beaks into th
water, ruffling their feathers and lending somethin
dignified to the scene that must be strange to ther
in their leisurely inspection of the canal and the rive
beyond. Jennifer watched, smiling. In this setting
she could be at ease with Nicholas Smythe. He wa
content to watch the swans, if the expression on hi
face was anything to go by. He broke the bread int
small pieces and she noticed the hands which, with
out rubber gloves, were as deft and gentle as ever.

He had held her in those strong arms when sh
fainted. He had carried her as if she was a chil
holding her close to his chest as if he feared to let he
go. He was the perfect, caring doctor, but what o
the man? She sighed.

'Not bored?' He looked surprised.

'No, I could do this for ever,' she said. 'You wer
right to come away from the hospital. It's a tempta
tion to stay and waste valuable free time, convincin
oneself that it is rest we need.' He was so close tha
his sleeve brushed against her bare arm. She too

some of the bread and moved away. His charisma of masculinity, his sudden gentleness were too much to bear.

'That's the lot,' he said. 'Look, the barges are coming up on the tide from the river.' He led her along the tow path where once heavy horses had strained on ropes to drag the strings of low-slung boats of goods and the river people who lived and died on the canals. They sat on a low wall and watched the greedy small waves dampen the bank as the boats came near. The evening breeze ruffled the dry heads of last year's grasses. ' "The sedge is withered by the lake and no bird sings." That's what the man said.'

'Do you know only the sad poems?' she said.

'There is a lot of sadness in the world,' he said, 'or hadn't you noticed? Sadness of our own making, if we stopped for a moment to look.' The dark eyes were sombre, the line of his mouth firm, almost as if he knew too much of sorrow.

'I heard that . . . you lost someone you loved . . . I'm sorry,' she said.

'You heard that I was in love with a woman who was pregnant by another man, she took drugs and was killed in a car crash. Is that what they say on the grapevine at Beatties?'

'Yes . . . but don't you mind, talking about it?'

'I would mind if it was all true. It's sad enough and I still mourn for a young and beautiful and very silly girl.'

'Is that fair, to speak of the dead like that, as if she was a stranger you pitied . . . rather than the woman you loved?'

'Did Beatties tell you that she was my your
cousin? That she had been a pain in the neck sin
she could walk but, although lovely and amusin
she was such a complete fool where men were co
cerned that we were all very fed up with her way
life.' He looked across the darkening water at t
lights bobbing on the other side. 'I did what I coul
at the risk of being called an interfering stuffed shir
but she wouldn't listen.'

'And you thought I was like her,' said Jennif
bitterly.

'I saw you first when you wore a mask. I saw th
your eyes were flecked with gold, like hers and
was a shock. I saw only your eyes and when you d
that rather stupid thing. . . .' He smiled. 'I though
that all girls with beautiful eyes must be the same.

'But you had no time for me when you saw m
again. Do you hate all women?'

'Everywhere I went I saw girls with beautiful eye
like hers. I saw her eyes the day before she die
when she swore that she wasn't pregnant, and th
clear light of honesty seemed unassailable. But sh
was lying, as only she could lie, looking me straig
in the face, the picture of injured innocence.'

'But I don't lie . . . only little white ones,' sai
Jennifer.

'Gradually, the three girls I saw at Beatti
became one. I saw the first one fit into the picture
the others today.'

'And were we all liars? Like her? Or do you no
believe me when I say that I am not pregnant,
have never slept with Nigel or any other man an
have no intention of doing so until I find a man wh

I can love and marry?' He bent his head from her scorn. 'You made my life miserable from the moment I first saw you,' she said. 'I could bear it when you were angry on the ward ... that is just one of the hazards of working with male chauvinists, but the other was ... unforgivable. I ... hated you,' she added, in a whisper. 'Almost as much as you seemed to hate me.'

He took both her hands and turned her to face him. 'I, hate *you*?' He gently shook her, 'I found you the most infuriating woman ... the most captivating, wilful, awkward girl I could hope to meet. I tried to dislike you, I was annoyed and fascinated and afraid to trust my inner conviction that you were beautiful, true, pure, and my own heart's love.'

He drew her unresisting body, as pliant as a reed by the water, into his arms. She gazed up at the dark, dark eyes in wonder. They had been stern, accusing, solemn and then, over the green mask in the theatre, they had told her something of his hidden feelings. They were full of such love and tenderness that she thought her heart would break with longing. His mouth was cool and hard on her trembling lips, the beat of his heart merged with her own as the turquoise silk was crushed between them.

And the river flowed on and the sedge blossomed again, and the swans mated once and for ever.

Look out for these three great Doctor Nurse Romances coming next month

CARIBBEAN NURSE
by Lydia Balmain

Staff Nurse Coral Summers' new job in the Caribbean is the chance of a lifetime, but couldn't she somehow have stopped herself falling in love with the arrogant surgeon Philip Kenning?

NURSE IN NEW MEXICO
by Constance Lea

Nurse Tessa Maitland flies all the way to Santa Fé and meets her sister's attractive doctor, Blair Lachlan. But she finds it hard to tell if he strongly dislikes her or is madly in love with her . . .

UNCERTAIN SUMMER
by Betty Neels

Nurse Serena Potts is thrilled when Dutchman Laurens van Amstel proposes to her, but the problems begin when he tries to back out of their engagement . . .

On sale where you buy Mills & Boon romances.

The Mills & Boon rose is the rose of romance

Mills & Boon
Best Seller Romances

The very best of Mills & Boon Romances
brought back for those of you who missed
them when they were first published.

In August
we bring back the following four
great romantic titles.

STORMY HAVEN
by Rosalind Brett

When Melanie came to the island of Mindoa in the Indian
Ocean she was little more than a schoolgirl; when she left,
only eight months later, she had grown into a woman. Her
scheming cousin Elfrida, Ramon Perez and the masterful
Stephen Brent had all played their parts in this transforma-
tion.

BOSS MAN FROM OGALLALA
by Janet Dailey

Casey knew she was perfectly capable of running her father's
ranch for him while he was in hospital. It was *only* because
she was a girl that Flint McCallister had been brought in to do
the job. So what with one thing and another, there was hardly
a warm welcome waiting for the new boss!

DARK CASTLE
by Anne Mather

What Julie had once felt for Jonas Hunter was now past
history and she had made every effort to keep it so. But now
she found herself travelling to Scotland to make contact with
him again. Could she manage to remain on purely business
terms with the man who had meant so much to her and whose
attraction for her had increased rather than lessened?

THE GIRL AT DANES' DYKE
by Margaret Rome

'Women aren't welcome at Danes' Dyke,' the inscrutable
Thor Halden told Raine; nevertheless circumstances forced
him to take her under his roof for a time, and to persuade her
to masquerade as his wife. It was a difficult enough situation
for Raine, even before she found herself falling in love with
him. Would she ever be able to make him trust her?

If you have difficulty in obtaining any of these books through
your local paperback retailer, write to:

Mills & Boon Reader Service
P.O. Box 236, Thornton Road, Croydon, Surrey, CR9 3RU.

Masquerade
Historical Romances

Intrigue excitement romance

BUCCANEER'S LADY
by Robyn Stuart

Corinna Barrett sailed to the West Indies to find her missing father, but she was kidnapped and sold as a slave to Captain Brandon Hawke before her search had really begun. Yet why had Brandon insisted on buying her, when he so clearly despised everything she stood for?

SUMMER HEIRESS
by Ann Hulme

Miss Aurelia Sinclair had just a year to save her Jamaican sugar estates from her father's creditors, and she was resolved to make a rich marriage. Unluckily, she fell in love with Harry, Viscount Belphege — who believed she was the heiress she had pretended to be!

Look out for these titles in your local paperback shop from 14th August 1981